D1233524

Coleen E. Booth was born and raised in
New York City. She attended the State
University of New York at Geneseo and
is a student at the New School for Social
Research. She is an adviser to the Junior
Youth Council of the NAACP and a volun-
teer Big Sister. *Going Live* is her first
novel.

GOING LIVE

GOING LIVE

Coleen E. Booth

CHARLES SCRIBNER'S SONS · NEW YORK
Maxwell Macmillan Canada · Toronto
Maxwell Macmillan International
New York · Oxford · Singapore · Sydney

Charles Scribner's Sons Books for Young Readers
Macmillan Publishing Company
866 Third Avenue, New York, NY 10022

Maxwell Macmillan Canada, Inc.
1200 Eglinton Avenue East, Suite 200
Don Mills, Ontario M3C 3N1

Macmillan Publishing Company is part of
the Maxwell Communication Group of Companies.

First Edition   10 9 8 7 6 5 4 3 2 1
Printed in the United States of America

Library of Congress Cataloging-in-Publication Data
Booth, Coleen E.
    Going live/Coleen E. Booth. — 1st ed.   p.   cm.
    Summary: A young television performer finds her private life
in conflict with her career.
    ISBN 0-684-19392-2
    [1. Television—Production and direction—Fiction.
2. Performing arts—Fiction. 3. Afro-Americans—Fiction.]   I. Title.
PZ7.B64635Go   1992   [Fic]—dc20   91-21607

To my mom and dad,
my sister, Lisa, and my brother, Derek,
with all my love.

• • • • • • •

And to my friend Samantha for her
encouragement and support

GOING LIVE

I

"Stop fidgeting, Delaney," Mom said to me as the taxi sped up Sixth Avenue. She reached over and fixed the scratchy collar on my blue dress. The city was hot and humid that day, and the patched-up vinyl seat was sticking to the back of my bare legs. "And where are the tights I told you to wear?"

"Mom, it's ninety degrees!" Only she would think of tights in the middle of a July heat wave. Besides, tights make me look shorter than I already am.

It was the second week of summer vacation, and I was determined to find a permanent acting assignment before school started. Surprisingly, Mom had even agreed to rearrange her schedule so she could take me on auditions. So far I had tried out for two soap operas, three nighttime comedies, and one Broadway play, but nothing had worked out for me yet.

When we reached the network building in Times Square, I slid out of the cab and waited impatiently as

Mom paid the fare. My head was pounding. Down the busy street there was a skyscraper that displayed the time, weather, and news headlines twenty-four hours a day in huge neon letters. It was 9:56. And I had been wrong. It was ninety-*three* degrees out there!

The network building is very New York. It's over sixty stories high and covered with mirrored glass, and in the lobby there's a great statue that looks like an ivory giraffe. I love it. Usually I like to take time to stare at it, but we had less than five minutes to get to the seventeenth floor.

Inside the crowded elevator Mom ran her hand down the side of my face and gave me a worried look. "How's your head?"

I shrugged. "All right."

She returned a short smile. "You're too young for these headaches. You have to stop putting all this pressure on yourself."

Easier said than done. Mom didn't know how important acting was to me. She thought I'd grow out of it one day.

But I wouldn't. I loved becoming new and interesting characters and seeing the world through their eyes for a little while. And even though acting was difficult, it was also fun. I couldn't imagine ever giving it up.

On Monday I had auditioned for a children's television show called "Friday Afternoon," and it had been a nerve-wracking experience. Not only was I the only black girl trying out, I was also the youngest. I must have done pretty well, though, because my agent, Mr. Kirby, phoned the next day and told Mom that the executive producer of the show, Ms. Seachman, wanted to meet with us. He said I had a good shot at getting this job.

But I wasn't as excited as I should have been because there were two problems with "Friday Afternoon" as far as I was concerned. Number one: the show had nothing to do with acting. It was some sort of talk show. Number two: the show would be aired live and that scared me. What if I made a mistake on camera?

The executive producer's office was huge, with two sofas, an Oriental rug, and tall windows overlooking Broadway.

"Please have a seat," Ms. Seachman said. She was standing in the doorway, obviously waiting for someone else.

"Thank you." As we sat down on one of the sofas, Mom whispered to me, "Have you ever seen a more impressive office?"

"Only on TV."

Soon a younger blond woman joined us. "This is Lauren Yarnell," Ms. Seachman said. "She is the production manager."

Mom gave Lauren the videotape we had been asked to bring. It had a few of my recent commercials and a clip from a television movie I had played a minor role in two years ago.

Lauren pushed it into a VCR. "We can talk while we watch," she said.

I started fidgeting again, and even though I knew I was doing it, I couldn't stop. I felt like a baby in my frilly dress with my shoulder-length brown hair combed back in blue barrettes.

Ms. Seachman asked Mom about my acting experience, and Mom went through the usual speech. She talked about how I got my first commercial when I was three years old, and how I landed a part in a miniseries when I was six. And on and on.

"Should we schedule her for a screen test?" Lauren asked Ms. Seachman after they had seen the entire videotape.

I crossed my fingers hoping she'd say no. Screen tests are like auditions in front of a camera, and they're really a pain in the neck.

"No. I think the video we just saw is good enough." Mrs. Seachman turned to me. "You've done some pretty good work, Delaney."

"Thank you."

Then she spent a few minutes explaining "Friday Afternoon" to me. She said they needed three kids to host a one-hour show every week. "The show is aimed at children eight to fourteen years old. And the majority of the work will involve interviewing celebrities, reviewing movies, records, and books, and some traveling."

"That sounds like a lot of responsibility," Mom said. "My daughter is only eleven years old."

"I understand your concern, Dr. Crawford, but the majority of the ideas will come from our staff. And the children will have plenty of time to rehearse before they go in front of the cameras. Not to mention an entire summer to attend speech classes." She looked at me again. "Delaney, if you were chosen as one of the hosts of 'Friday Afternoon,' do you think you'd be able to handle it?"

I didn't know what to say. Mr. Kirby had told me that the job had been designed for a teenager, but after hearing what the show was about, I wanted to be a part of it more than ever. So, in my most mature-sounding voice, I said, "Sure. I think it'd be great!"

· · · · · · ·

"What are you going to do this afternoon?" Mom asked me while we were having lunch at home. She didn't think I was old enough to stay in our brownstone apartment alone. "Do you want to come to the office with me or go visit Tasha?"

Mom's a dentist, and she and a colleague, Dr. Cahill, started their own practice a year ago. I didn't want to go to her office because the last time I was there, Mom asked Dr. Cahill to give me a checkup and a cleaning. Ugh!

"I'll go see if Kelly is around," I said, finishing up the last of my salad. I didn't want Mom to know that Tasha and I weren't speaking to each other.

"Okay. I'd better run. Give me a call and let me know where you are. And if Kelly isn't at home, come on over to the office."

"All right." The clinic is on Tenth Street, only two blocks away, so she doesn't mind if I walk there by myself. She just doesn't want me on the block without anyone to play with.

Kelly lived down the street in another brownstone. Even before I rang the bell, I could hear the rock music blaring through the window. Mrs. O'Shea opened the door and walked me down the hall to their first-floor apartment.

When I stepped into the living room, I was surprised to see Tasha there. She and Kelly weren't really good friends. The only thing they had in common was me. But there they were, watching MTV together.

· 5 ·

"Kelly, would you turn that down!" Mrs. O'Shea shouted above the music. "I just put Lynn down for a nap."

Kelly turned the volume down before she noticed me. "Oh, Laney!" she said. "I didn't see you there." As usual Kelly was dressed in a great pink outfit. She had more pink things than I had things at all. Pink clips held her long blond hair in a ponytail, and she was wearing bright pink hi-top sneakers.

Tasha gave me a dirty look. Against her brown skin, her dark eyes looked mean and piercing. When Tasha wasn't steamed she was the prettiest girl I knew. And she already had a figure like a woman.

The tension in the room was so thick I wanted to just turn around and leave, but I wasn't about to give Tasha the satisfaction, so instead I took a seat next to Kelly on the floor and stared at the TV as a Billy Denim video came on.

"I called your house a little while ago," Kelly told me. "Did you and your mother go out for brunch?"

Kelly is really into food, and every week we get together to cook lunch. The week before we had made broccoli quiche. Today I had hoped she and I would plan next week's meal, but that was impossible with Tasha there.

"No, I had a meeting with a producer."

I tried to make it sound as if it was nothing special, but I could hear Tasha mumble under her breath, "Big deal."

She always acted that way when I mentioned auditions or commercials.

"Why don't you stop being so jealous, Tasha?" I asked.

"Why don't you stop bragging?" She stood up over me.

I jumped up, too, but of course I couldn't match her

height. "I'm not bragging! Kelly asked me where I was, so I told her. You're the one with the problem!"

Kelly squeezed in between us. "Would you two stop it? My little sister's asleep, and I don't want my mother coming in here." She pulled me away from Tasha and sat me down on the couch. "Come on, Laney. Seriously."

"Sure, Kelly. Blame me!"

Kelly stamped her foot. "I'm not blaming you. I just don't want to get in trouble."

"Everything was fine until you came, Delaney," Tasha cried. "You should have just stayed away!" With that she stormed out of the room. The front door slammed a few seconds later, and the baby began crying in another room.

Mrs. O'Shea shrieked, "Kelly, I told you to be quiet!" She sounded very annoyed, and I knew it was half my fault. Inside I wished I hadn't even come over to Kelly's. I probably would have had more fun at Mom's office getting my teeth drilled.

· · · · · · ·

Later that evening while I was playing Super Mario Bros. in our den, I heard the telephone ring in the kitchen. I ran to get it before the second ring because Mom was meditating in her bedroom.

"Laney? It's Parker Kirby. Is your mother home?" Mr. Kirby has to be one of the fastest-talking humans on the face of the earth.

"Yes, but she's meditating. Is it an emergency or anything?" It had to be about the producer's decision, but I couldn't tell from his tone if it was good news or bad. I was dying!

"No, don't bother her. I can give you the information and she can phone me tomorrow." He took a breath. "Ms. Seachman called. She picked the three kids for the show."

My heart actually stopped. His voice sounded as if he was going into his better-luck-next-time speech.

"You got it, kid!"

I screamed right in his ear. Then I remembered that Mom needed quiet, and I whispered. "Oh wow! I can't believe it!"

"She said your videotape was extraordinary. And she loved your confidence."

Then he told me that Mom and I had to meet with Ms. Seachman at ten o'clock the next Monday. I was so ecstatic when I hung up that I ran into Mom's room, bursting to tell her the good news. She was still on the floor with her legs crossed in lotus position and her eyes closed.

I flopped on her queen-size bed with a huge smile pasted to my lips. I couldn't believe it! They liked me even though I'm only eleven.

And so what if this show didn't have any acting in it? This would be my first *real* television job and I'd get to do what I loved every single week. What could be better than that?

When Mom finished meditating, she stretched out on the floor and smiled when she saw me on her bed. "When are you going to let me teach you how to meditate?" she asked. "It might end all your headaches."

Headaches were the last thing on my mind. "Guess what?"

She sat up. "Good news or bad news?"

"Good news."

She stared at me, trying to read my thoughts. Then she threw her head back and laughed. "You got 'Friday Afternoon'!"

"How did you guess it?" I hopped onto the floor, and Mom grabbed me and gave me a big hug.

"I'm psychic," she said, and flooded me with kisses.

· · · · · · ·

At dinner that night Mom got serious. "First of all," she began, "I want you to know how proud I am of you."

"Thank you." I still had that smile on my face.

"But I want you to think about this long and hard, Delaney. Are you sure you want to do this? *Really* sure?"

I nodded immediately. "Yes, I am."

Mom shook her head. "No. I want you to take your time before you make this decision. This is not a commercial that will be over in one day. This is a long-term job that will need all of your concentration. You will be rehearsing a great deal, and you won't have as much time for your friends. And you won't be able to go away to camp this summer."

"I don't care. I want to do it."

Mom passed me the dish of stir-fry vegetables with almonds. "Tell me why you want to do it."

"Well, I like being on TV, and it seems like a good way to boost my career." There. That was the honest answer.

"That's not good enough."

I knew what she was getting at. I had done a ton of commercials, and I had never had the same enthusiasm about them. This was different. "I like the idea behind this show, Mom. And I can learn a lot from being a part of this."

"And you won't mind sacrificing some things for it?"

I shook my head. "I know I'm going to have to give up a lot of things, and I know I'm going to miss the free time I have now, but I think it'll be worth it."

2

Mom knocked on my door early on Monday morning. "It's eight o'clock, Delaney," she said cheerfully. Mom is a morning person.

"I'm up," I said, but I really wasn't. My eyes were having a hard time adjusting to the light streaming in through the window. The night before had been torture. For hours I had tossed and turned, unable to sleep, worrying about what the other two kids on the show would be like.

"Delaney!"

"I'm coming, I'm coming!"

I opened my eyes and stared ahead at the framed picture of Mom, Dad, and me hanging on my wall. I love that picture. It always gives me inspiration. It had been taken while we were vacationing in Kenya when I was only three years old, and in the background stood a beautiful giraffe. We were all happy then.

Four years after that picture was taken, Dad died in a

car crash. He had been hit by a drunk driver. Even though I was only seven at the time, I remember the day he died as if it was yesterday. I didn't understand how that woman could drink alcohol and then get behind the wheel of a car. She had taken Dad away from me.

After Dad died my whole life changed and it seemed as though nothing would ever be right again. For a long time I felt empty inside. Sometimes I still feel that way. Not a day goes by that I don't miss Dad. Not one.

The reason the photograph inspires me is that Dad took me to my first audition around that same time, and he always encouraged me to act. If it hadn't been for him, I never would have known how great performing could be. In a way, acting made me feel closer to him.

"You don't want us to be late, do you?" Mom asked, standing in my doorway.

"We won't be."

"Well, hurry up. I'm making oatmeal for breakfast."

I sat up. "Oatmeal? Mom, it's the middle of the summer!"

She laughed. "See, I know exactly how to get you up!"

· · · · · · ·

We arrived at the network building a few minutes before ten o'clock. Mr. Kirby was waiting outside Ms. Seachman's office, nervously looking at his watch.

"I thought you'd be late," he said to Mom in his usual speedy manner. He was dressed in a bright red sport coat and brown polyester pants. Mom always says he has terrible fashion sense. She thinks he gets his clothes from the Salvation Army. He kissed Mom on the cheek. "I was beginning to think Laney had second thoughts about all this."

Mr. Kirby hardly ever talked directly to me when Mom was around.

Inside the office Ms. Seachman and Lauren greeted us. Lauren put her arm around my shoulder and led me outside and down the hallway. "While the grown-ups discuss business, let me introduce you to the other kids."

Oh, boy. The moment of truth.

First I met Cory Drennen, who was standing by the watercooler with his mother. He wasn't the best-looking boy I'd ever met, but he had a cute smile and freckles. And he was extremely friendly. I found out that he was thirteen years old and lived in New Jersey.

"How long does it take to get here from your house?" I asked.

"It's supposed to take about a half hour, but with my mother driving me, it took over an hour. She's a nervous wreck."

Lauren tapped me on the shoulder. "Let's go meet Kathleen. You'll be sharing a dressing room with her."

Kathleen was a beautiful teenager with long red hair and bright green eyes. We shook hands. "Hi," she said with a big smile. "I'm Kathleen Sutherland. I'm on the cover of *Seventeen* this month."

What did she want? A medal? "Hi, I'm Delaney Crawford."

The dressing room was pretty large, with a sofa, a love seat, two makeup tables with lighted mirrors, and a coffee table with a telephone on it. A door in the back of the room led to a bathroom with a shower.

"You probably saw me on 'Entertainment Tonight' last year," Kathleen continued. "My mother is Diana Sutherland. They did a segment on the children of famous movie stars."

"I must have missed that episode," I said, trying to be polite.

"You two girls get acquainted," Lauren said. "And I'll go see if Ms. Seachman needs me for anything."

"Don't worry," Kathleen said. "I'll take good care of little Delaney."

I took a seat at one of the makeup tables and tried to find the switch to turn on the lights. As soon as Lauren was out of sight, Kathleen's smile disappeared. She tossed her hair and shot me a mean look. "Okay, let's get something straight," she said. "The sofa is mine and the love seat is yours. And this is my makeup table. If I ever catch you going through my stuff, you're in big trouble, little girl."

I was stunned into silence.

"Another thing," she added. "I'm the star around here. Understand?"

I stared at her. *She* wasn't the star of the show. All *three* of us were. But for some reason I couldn't talk.

When Lauren came back to the dressing room, Kathleen returned to being nice. The girl was definitely an actress.

"Delaney, come with me," Lauren said. "Ms. Seachman wants to see you."

In the office Mom and Mr. Kirby were at Ms. Seachman's desk. I leaned over Mom's shoulder to see what she was doing, but she was just signing a bunch of papers.

Ms. Seachman smiled up at me. "I just wanted to welcome you, Delaney," she said. "I'm sure we all can work together very well. Do you like your dressing room?"

"Yes, thank you. It's very nice." I felt a rush of excitement all of a sudden. I couldn't believe I was actually there.

· · · · · · ·

"So, tell me, how did it go?" Kelly asked the moment I stepped into her apartment. It was about three hours later, and it had begun to rain, a sun-shower. I was practically soaked standing there carrying a heavy grocery bag full of everything we needed for Italian stuffed shells.

I laughed. "Would you give me a chance to get in the door? Gosh!" I walked quickly past her into the kitchen and laid the heavy bag on the counter with a sigh of relief.

Kelly followed me, waiting for my response. "Well?"

"Okay, okay," I said. "It went all right, I guess." Then I thought about Kathleen and added, "But the girl I share a dressing room with is a bossy, stuck-up airhead."

"Is she better or worse than Gina Foster?" Gina is a girl at school who only cares about how she looks and what boy she's going out with.

"Gina is nice compared to Kathleen." I went to the sink and washed my hands. "It ees time to cook!" I declared in my best Italian accent.

"We can't use the oven until my mother gets back from the cleaner's," Kelly said. "She left me here baby-sitting Lynn."

Lucky her! Her mother lets her baby-sit for her sister, and mine won't even let me sit for myself yet. "No problem. We can prepare zee shells."

The two of us worked hard for about fifteen minutes

boiling the pasta shells and seasoning the ricotta cheese. When the shells were soft enough, we had to fill them with the cheese, and it was sort of difficult. If you weren't careful, the shell would tear. Kelly and I ended up with eleven good shells and a whole bunch of useless pieces.

"I hope your mother gets home soon," I said.

"Me too. It's almost three-thirty and my sister is going to need to be fed."

"Why don't *we* feed her?"

"We can't. Mom's breast-feeding her."

"Well, can we take a look at her?" Lynn was already five weeks old, and I had only seen her once.

We tiptoed down the hallway and into her mother's bedroom. "Excuse the mess," Kelly whispered as we crept toward the crib.

Baby clothes and sheets were folded up all over Mr. and Mrs. O'Shea's bed. On the floor boxes of diapers and baby toys lined the walls. "Most of these were gifts Mom got at the baby shower."

Lynn was sound asleep and breathing heavily. She was so tiny, with the cutest little red face, framed by thin wisps of blond hair. Her little hands were balled up in wrinkled fists. I sighed. "She's beautiful. She's going to look just like you when she grows up."

Kelly giggled. "No. She's going to be much prettier."

The baby stirred a little, and we sucked in our breaths and stood absolutely still. A few moments later she fell back into a sound sleep. I couldn't take my eyes off her. She was perfect.

"We better leave before she starts crying," Kelly said. "She's small, but she has big lungs!"

While we waited for Mrs. O'Shea, Kelly and I did something we had been planning for a long time. We made friendship bracelets for each other.

I used little pink and white beads for Kelly's. I put them on a piece of string and tied it onto her wrist. It looked pretty. "Now you have to promise never to take it off," I said.

She held up her hand. "I promise."

Then she put a yellow-and-white one on my wrist. "Now you promise."

"I promise," I said. "Does this mean we'll stay friends for life?"

Kelly nodded. "No matter what."

· · · · · · ·

That night while Kelly and I were on the phone, I couldn't concentrate because Mom kept asking, "Didn't you two spend the whole afternoon together? What more could you possibly have to say to each other?"

"Hold on, Kelly." I turned to Mom. "Guess what? I can't hear her." I was on shaky ground. Sometimes she lets me get away with saying things like that to her. Sometimes not.

Mom gave me a funny look. "Whose phone is it?"

"Yours," I mumbled, getting the message. Then I heard a click in the phone. "Kelly, would you mind holding? There's another call coming in."

The call was from Mom's partner, Dr. Cahill, so I had to say good-bye to Kelly and give the phone to Mom, who asked me for privacy.

I went into the den and turned on the TV, but really I

was dying to eavesdrop on their telephone conversation. From the look on Mom's face, I didn't think they were going to talk about some patient's root canal.

I turned the sound down and tiptoed over to the doorway where I was able to see and hear Mom through the crack. She was smiling from ear to ear.

"Saturday night?" she asked. "I don't know. I'll have to find a sitter for Delaney. . . . I know but—" She laughed. And this wasn't a normal, everyday kind of laugh. This was a woman-interested-in-a-man laugh. "Okay, okay. Saturday sounds just fine. . . . That will be nice. I'll see you tomorrow at the office. I'm glad you called, Joshua. Bye-bye."

Bye-bye? I'd never heard Mom say that before. As she stood to hang up the phone, I ran back over to the TV and turned up the volume. When Mom stuck her head in the doorway, I was sitting on the floor looking as innocent as Kelly's baby sister.

But Mom wasn't buying it. "Hear anything good lately?" she asked me.

"Should I have?"

She came into the den and took a seat next to me on the floor. "Well, since you already heard, tell me what you think."

"About you dating Dr. Cahill?"

She nodded and folded her legs.

I took a deep breath. "I don't know. Do you like him?"

She smiled. "Yes, I do. We've been having sort of lunch dates these last couple of weeks. Now he wants to take me out to dinner."

I liked Dr. Cahill. He was funny and handsome and he had a great Australian accent. But Dr. Cahill was white.

· 18 ·

"I don't think you should date him, Mom. Everyone's going to stare at you."

Mom's eyes took on a hurt look. "Delaney, I don't care about that. And neither does Joshua."

I shrugged. "It looks like you've already made up your mind. Why are you asking me, then?"

"Because I want you to approve. I want you to be happy with this."

I wasn't happy. I was angry. What about Dad? One date with Dr. Cahill would probably lead to another and another and she would wind up forgetting all about Dad.

Besides why would Mom want to date somebody who was a different race? Wouldn't that just make things harder? "If I don't approve, will that stop you from dating him?"

Mom paused for a moment. Then she said, "No."

"Fine, then. Do whatever you like." I got up and walked out of the den. I had never thought about Mom dating anyone, and I didn't want to start now. I had figured she would go on loving Dad forever. I guess I was wrong.

• • • • • • •

When I came out to the kitchen the next morning, Mom was already on the phone with you-know-who. She was at the counter, wiping off the juicer and balancing the phone between her ear and shoulder.

"Is there any breakfast?" I asked.

She pointed to the stove but didn't stop talking.

On the stove was an omelet with cheese and green peppers. "Have you eaten already?"

She nodded at me, but said to him, "That sounds nice."

"Where's the juice?"

Mom pointed to the refrigerator. I pulled open the door. There were two quart-sized bottles of fresh juice. "What kind of juices are these, Mom?"

"Hold on one moment, Joshua," she said. "Delaney just woke up." She covered the mouthpiece with her hand and turned to me. "You're being a brat, Delaney. Now what's the problem?"

"I just want to know if you made orange-pineapple juice, that's all. You didn't have to put your precious call on hold for *me*."

Mom went back to the conversation and quickly ended it, telling Dr. Cahill she would see him later at the office. When she got off the phone, she told me to have a seat.

I flung myself onto a counter stool dramatically. "Okay?"

She stared at me. "I want to know why you found it necessary to interrupt my conversation."

I shrugged. "You weren't talking about anything important, were you?"

"What I was talking about is not the issue here. When I'm on the phone, you will patiently wait until I am finished. Is that clear?"

I nodded.

"I don't like your attitude this morning, young lady. Dr. Cahill is a dear friend of mine and a business partner. And you will show him nothing but respect." Mom's tone was sterner than I ever remember.

"Yes, Mom." I sat there for a few more minutes with my arms folded over my chest. Mom and Dr. Cahill hadn't even gone on a real date yet, and she was changing already.

3

Our first rehearsal was that morning. We were all herded into a room that was completely empty except for wall-to-wall carpeting.

"Welcome to your second home," Lauren said.

"But there's no furniture!" Kathleen cried.

"Who needs furniture?"

Kathleen leaned against the wall. "There's no way I'm going to sit on the floor in my new skirt."

"Then you'll be standing the entire day," Lauren told her. Then she turned to Cory and me. "Make yourselves comfortable. We have a lot to cover today."

Cory and I sat on the floor near the window. Kathleen remained standing.

"Doesn't she know how to dress for rehearsal?" Cory whispered to me.

The rest of us, including Lauren, were wearing jeans, T-shirts, and sneakers. Kathleen looked as if she was going to the Plaza for lunch.

First Lauren handed us our schedules for the rest of the summer. We had to be there at nine o'clock, have lunch from eleven-thirty to one, then work until four.

"I won't be able to make it on Thursday," Kathleen said. "I'm doing a photo layout for *Sassy* magazine."

Again Lauren ignored her. "Now I know Ms. Seachman explained the show to each of you, and as we get into rehearsals you'll learn more about it. But do any of you have any questions?"

I raised my hand. "Ms. Seachman mentioned traveling. Where to?"

"All over. For our first show we're going to spend a weekend on a fossil dig upstate and tape a segment there."

That sounded like fun, but Mom would never let me travel once school started. Not if it meant being absent.

"Can we have a back-to-school fashion show?" Kathleen asked. She was still leaning against the wall with her arms folded.

"That sounds like a good idea. I'll see what Ms. Seachman thinks about it."

"Where's the studio where we'll do the show?" Cory asked.

"We'll be using the small studio down the corridor. It's under construction now." She walked around the room and handed out another sheet of paper. This one was a calendar and September fourth was circled. "The period of time from today until we tape our first segment is called preproduction. As you can see from this calendar, we have exactly seven weeks of preproduction. By the way, we have a big surprise lined up for that first show."

I leaned forward. "What kind of surprise?"

"I can't tell you. Ms. Seachman will kill me if I let it slip."

"Let what slip?" Cory asked slyly.

"Good try, squirt."

Then we spent five minutes guessing. Even Kathleen got into the act. But Lauren wouldn't even tell us when we were getting warm or cold.

Lauren held up her hands. "Calm down, troops. Maybe I shouldn't have said anything."

The next paper she handed us looked like some kind of NASA calculations. "Okay, this is a sample of the show rundown, which you will be given every week. I know this may look a little confusing at first, but—"

"A little!" I exclaimed.

"Don't worry, Delaney. In a few minutes this will all be a piece of cake."

Actually, she was right. Once we got past all the numbers, symbols, and abbreviations, it became clear that it was just a list explaining the order of the show's events. First there was the opening, then the introductions of the hosts, then the first story, then commercial number one, etc. To be honest, being able to understand it made me feel very professional.

Kathleen asked, "What will we be doing for seven weeks?"

"You'll be taking speech classes, and I'll be going over the skills you will need to put this type of show together. Seven weeks isn't really that long."

Kathleen sulked. "There goes my trip to Tahiti."

Lauren shook her head. "Nobody's forcing you to do this show, Kathleen. It's up to you."

"I'm here, right?"

Cory and I looked at each other. She had some attitude.

"The first thing we'll be videotaping is a promo for 'Friday Afternoon'," Lauren said.

"What's a promo?" Cory asked.

"It's a short commercial that will let everyone know about our show. We're trying to get that set up for next week."

"So soon?" I asked. I didn't know whether to feel excited or scared.

· · · · · · ·

We took a ten-minute break around ten-thirty because Lauren had to meet with Ms. Seachman. The three of us stayed in the rehearsal room asking one another about our acting experience. Kathleen had had a walk-on part in one of her mother's movies when she was young. Cory was a beginner, but he had studied acting with some well-known British instructor. I had the most experience, even though most of it was in commercials.

When Lauren came back, she told us to quiet down because Ms. Seachman wanted her to go over some important things with us.

"Like what?" Kathleen asked, sounding bored.

"Well, like reminding you to respect one another's privacy. She doesn't want any visiting between dressing rooms."

Kathleen sighed loudly.

"Another thing," Lauren continued. "They tape 'The Business Review' show down the hall from us. Those people are extremely serious, and I don't have to tell you that they weren't too happy when they found out that a bunch of adolescents were going to share a floor with them. So let's not have any loud noises in the hallway or playing around by the elevators. Arrive here on time each morning and behave professionally all day. Get it?"

Cory said, "Got it."

I said, "Yeah."

We all looked at Kathleen. She rolled her eyes to the ceiling. "Okay, okay. Don't make a federal case out of it."

Next we had to meet with Penny, the wardrobe woman, to get measured. My measurements were a disgrace. Sometimes I wondered if I would ever get a real figure like Tasha or Kathleen.

We spent the rest of the morning touring the executive offices and meeting the associate producers and all the people who were working on the show. By the time we were finished it was eleven-fifteen, almost time for lunch. Mom had given me money to buy something, but she said I couldn't leave the building alone.

I stopped at the watercooler next to the elevator. My mouth had gone dry from having to say hello to all those people. Then I walked down the carpeted hallway toward the dressing room to get my knapsack. I tried the knob. It was locked. Inside I could hear Kathleen talking to somebody on the phone.

I knocked and waited, but she didn't respond. So I knocked again, louder this time. Still there was no answer.

"Kathleen! Open up, it's me."

From the other side of the door I heard, "Go away!"

"I have just as much right to be in there as you do!"

"I said, get lost!"

I kicked the door. That girl had problems, but if she

thought she was going to take advantage of me, she was sadly mistaken.

I walked down the hallway to Cory's dressing room. The door was open, and he was sitting on the floor eating a sandwich.

I stood in the entrance and said, "Knock knock."

"Laney. Come in."

"What about the rules?"

"Oh, yeah. Want to go eat in the rehearsal room?"

I held up my empty hands. "My lunch money is in my dressing room, and Kathleen locked me out."

He stood up. "Let's go tell Lauren. We can't let her get away with this."

"Yeah!"

Lauren was in her office talking on the phone. "May I help you two?" she asked, covering the mouthpiece with her hand.

"Kathleen locked Laney out of her dressing room."

"I'll be there in a minute." She took her hand away. "Eric, I have to go now. The kids are having a problem."

The three of us walked down the hallway. But when Lauren turned the doorknob, the door opened with ease. She gave me a suspicious look.

"It was locked a few minutes ago," I protested. "Honestly."

Kathleen came to the door. "What seems to be the problem?" She looked completely innocent with her eyes opened wide. I felt silly standing there. And mad. What was she trying to do? Make me look like a fool?

· · · · · · ·

When Mom picked me up at four, I was still fuming, not to mention starving. I had been too upset to eat at lunchtime. At home I went straight from the front door to the refrigerator. "Mom, there's nothing to eat!"

Mom started digging inside the fridge. She pulled out three dishes of food. "What do you mean there's nothing to eat? What do you call all of this?"

I sighed.

"Sit down, Delaney. Allow me to fix something for my working daughter. In the meantime drink some milk."

I was too tired to argue, so I drank the milk. Then I asked, "Did you go to lunch with *him* again today?"

"Yes, why?"

"Never mind."

We were quiet for a little longer. Mom busied herself with making dinner. Finally she broke the silence. "How did it go today?"

"Okay. Lauren gave us our schedules for the rest of the summer. It's hectic. I won't have time to do anything else, except on weekends."

Mom leaned over and kissed my forehead. "Then we'll just have to make your weekends extra fun."

4

. . . .

"Doesn't my hair look terrific this way?" Kathleen asked on Friday. She was seated in her favorite spot, in front of the lighted mirror. "They teased it yesterday for my photo layout. I think I can pass for seventeen this way."

"You still look fourteen to me," I said.

"What would a baby like you know?" She stood up. "Gosh, this bra is really annoying. But you wouldn't know anything about that, would you?"

"Why don't you shut up?"

"Is the baby getting mad?" she teased.

Even though I knew she was trying to get to me, I felt angry at her for being such a self-centered witch. And angry at myself for letting her hurt me.

Our break was over, and we hurried to the rehearsal room for our speech class. Mariella, our teacher, was waiting for us. "Come along, children. We do not have time to waste." She was a good teacher, but not a very patient one.

We stood side by side facing her.

"Okay, everybody. Let us begin by breathing in and out deeply. I want to *hear* you breathe."

We always began like this.

"I do not hear you, Miss Crawford," she said.

I breathed louder.

"Very good."

When we had done that for a few minutes, she asked us to repeat after her. "Speak the speech, I pray you. As I pronounced it to you. Trippingly on the tongue." She rolled her *r*'s and rounded her *o*'s.

We giggled.

"How can you laugh at Shakespeare? Please repeat after me."

We did what she asked. Then she made us do it again and again until she heard each and every letter. "You have to forget the way you speak in the street and project each word clearly. Now I want each of you to say it alone. Miss Sutherland, you may begin."

Kathleen walked to the front of the room and started, "Speak the—"

"Miss Sutherland," Mariella interrupted. "I would think that as a model, your posture would be better. Now stand up straight."

Cory laughed.

"Mr. Drennen. Please. What Miss Sutherland lacks in posture, she makes up for in speaking ability. You, on the other hand, have a very heavy New Jersey accent that will need some undoing."

"What's a New Jersey accent?" Cory wanted to know.

I remained silent out of fear.

There was a knock on the door and Lauren popped in.

"Sorry to interrupt, Mariella. Kathleen, I just spoke with Ms. Seachman. She approved your idea for the back-to-school fashion show."

"Terrific!"

"We'll have a meeting right after lunch to come up with some other ideas."

At eleven-thirty Lauren's boyfriend, Eric Flynn, came to take her out to lunch. Kathleen went shopping with some teenage soap opera actors who worked in our building, and Cory's father came to take him to the dermatologist. He'd gotten a pimple, and he was worried that he would get more.

Since I couldn't leave the building by myself, I went downstairs to the commissary on the fourth floor. It was crowded and I couldn't find a seat, so I brought my bowl of salad back upstairs and ate in my dressing room. Alone.

· · · · · · ·

That evening while I lay on the sofa half sleeping, half watching a rerun of "Family Ties," Mom talked to Tasha's mother on the phone. They were discussing a curtain sale at A&S. I could hardly keep my eyes open.

Then I heard Mom say, "Sure, I'd be glad to go with you. Delaney and I will be ready in fifteen minutes."

I couldn't believe my ears. "Mom, why do I have to go?"

"Because you're eleven years old, and I expect you to do as I say."

"Great answer, Mom! Don't you think you're being just a little insensitive? Or is shopping with Mrs. Graham more important than your own child?"

"Put your shoes on," she said calmly. "And watch the tone of voice you use when you talk to me."

I sulked all the way up the street.

"You might as well make the best of it," Mom said. "And I don't want you acting up in front of Mrs. Graham."

And then, if things weren't bad enough, guess who was standing outside the house with her mother? Tasha.

"Lisa, thanks for coming with me on such short notice," Mrs. Graham told Mom.

Tasha and I glared at each other. Apparently Tasha didn't want her mother to know we weren't speaking either. So as we walked to the corner to hail a taxi, the two of us didn't say a single word.

Mom and Mrs. Graham looked at every swatch of fabric and every style of curtain in the entire department store. Mom wanted me to stay close to her, but when she wasn't looking I inched away toward the toy department where they had rows and rows of giant stuffed animals.

For some reason Tasha followed me. "You better not say a word to my mother," she warned.

"Why don't you just stay away from me?" I asked. "We have nothing to say to each other, and that's just fine with me."

"Me too." Tasha spun around to walk away, but she tripped on my foot and fell to the carpeted floor with a thud. "Ow," she said, rubbing her elbow. She looked up at me furiously. "You did that on purpose, didn't you?"

I started to defend myself, but there was no way I could ever convince her that it had been an accident.

A salesperson helped her up. "Are you all right, young lady?" he asked.

"I think so."

"Where are your parents?"

"My mother is over there with the curtains. I'm all right, though."

When he left, Tasha pointed her finger at me. "Don't think you're going to get away with this, Delaney, because you're not! You just started a war!"

· · · · · · ·

Even though it was Saturday, I woke up at seven o'clock and spent the whole morning watching cartoons. Then around noon I went into Mom's room and phoned Kelly and told her what had happened the night before.

"I can't believe Tasha acted that way. She actually declared war?"

"Those were her exact words."

"Sometimes she acts so stupid," Kelly said. "I can't believe I'm going to have to spend a whole month away at camp with her. I wish you were going."

I sighed. "Me too." For the first time I felt left out.

"It's going to be boring without you. Remember the play we put on last year, *The Three Little Kittens*?"

I laughed. Our cabin had put on little skits for the younger campers. Tasha, Kelly, and I had dressed up in kitten costumes and pranced around on stage crying because we had lost our mittens. "It was ridiculous."

"Yeah, but we had fun."

We all had gone to Camp Sycamore for three years in a row and we had had some of the best times of our lives there. For one thing we were away from home and out of the city. And of course our parents weren't there, so we were free. And there were so many things to do—swimming and diving competitions, arts and crafts, scavenger hunts, movies, scary stories around the campfire, and my favorite, the plays.

"When are you leaving?" I asked.

"Next Friday. I really wish you were coming."

"Me too," I repeated.

"Delaney, can you come over now? I want you to see my room. My mother and I painted it yesterday."

"What color?"

"Pink."

"Wasn't it pink before?"

"Well, before it was powder-puff pink and now it's carnation pink."

I laughed. "I'll ask my mother if I can come over."

"Hurry up. I haven't seen you for so long."

"Okay, give me ten minutes."

· · · · · · · ·

I spent the afternoon with Kelly trying to redecorate her bedroom now that it was painted a "new" color. She had bought a whole lot of posters of movie stars, and she couldn't decide which hunk she wanted next to her bed. The choice was narrowed down to three when Mom called to tell me to come home.

While she got ready for her date, I sat in the den watching some stupid game show on TV. I was bored, and the evening ahead of me didn't look any brighter. Mom probably had hired some baby-sitter to come over, and she wouldn't do anything but eat all our food and talk on the phone with her boyfriend. Fun, fun, fun!

Mom must have been reading my mind because she came into the den at that moment, smiling. "I have a surprise for you."

"What is it?"

"Well . . ." She was stalling on purpose. "To begin with, I didn't call a baby-sitter for you tonight."

Finally! Mom had realized that I was old enough to be in the apartment by myself. This was a big day in the Crawford household. I had been freed from the baby-sitter prison.

"Mrs. Graham and I were talking yesterday about how you and Tasha haven't had a chance to spend much time together this summer. So she decided to surprise Tasha by inviting you over to spend the night with her tonight. Isn't that terrific?"

I couldn't believe this was happening to me. Mom was looking at me waiting for my reaction. "Great, Mom," I said in a flat voice. "Just great."

• • • • • • •

I rang Tasha's doorbell and stood outside in the darkness. For the life of me, I couldn't believe Mom had forced me into this mess just so she could go on a date. The funny part was, she actually thought she was doing me a favor.

Mrs. Graham came to the door. "Delaney, you're just in time for dinner."

I walked down the hallway and followed Mrs. Graham into the dining room with my knapsack still over my shoulder.

Tasha and her three brothers were at the dinner table with their father and everyone seemed to be talking at the same time. Sometimes I wish I had a big family. I mean, even though my home is much more peaceful, it seems like Tasha's family has a lot more fun.

Mr. Graham pulled a chair up to the table for me. "Come in, Delaney. My wife has made her famous roast beef." I loved his West Indian accent even though I didn't always understand everything he said.

"Delaney is a vegetarian," Tasha said sullenly.

"I remembered all about that, Tasha," Mrs. Graham said, getting a bowl from the cabinet. "That's why I prepared something special for Delaney."

The special dinner was kidney bean soup with dumplings. It tasted good, with an unusual flavor. I guess since Tasha's parents are from Jamaica, they use different spices. I wished Mom knew how to make it.

After dinner the family went into the living room to watch a movie they had rented. I sat on one side of the room and Tasha on the other. I glanced at my watch. It wasn't even eight-thirty. Time was just crawling by.

The movie was *The Wild Land,* and it was an action movie set in the future. The boys loved it. So did I, but I had to keep explaining what was going on to George, Tasha's eight-year-old brother.

When the movie ended, everyone went to their bedrooms. "You take the bed," Tasha said closing the door behind her. "I'll sleep on the floor."

"*I'll* sleep on the floor. Don't do me any favors."

"Fine." She gave me a mean look, then flopped down on her bed. "I don't know why my mother invited you. *I* certainly don't want you here."

I snatched the pillow off her bed and threw it on the

floor. "Don't worry. I'll be gone at the crack of dawn." I struggled to pull the blanket from underneath her. When it finally gave, I balled it up in my arms. "I'll go sleep on the couch." I picked up the pillow and my knapsack.

Tasha jumped up and blocked the door. "You're not going anywhere!"

"Yes, I am!" I tried to push her away, but the blanket got in the way. I wound up falling against the door and Tasha.

"Ow!" she cried, holding her side. "I hate you, Delaney. I really do!"

There was a knock on the door. "Tasha?" It was Mr. Graham.

"Yes, Daddy?"

"It's late. Would you two girls stop playing around?" His stern voice always had the same effect on me. It frightened me as well as made me long for my own father. When I was little and used to act up, just hearing Dad's voice would make me behave.

"I'm sorry, Daddy." She put her finger to her lips and warned me, "If you try something like that again, I'm going to—"

"What are you going to do?" I folded my arms across my chest, tempting her to try something.

Just then the door flew open and George ran in. "I need help, Tasha. Troy is going to kill me!"

I laughed, letting go of some of the hostility I was feeling. George was really cute. "Get under the bed," I said.

He dropped to the floor and crawled underneath. Tasha picked up the blanket and laid it over the bed so he was completely hidden.

"Where is he?" Troy demanded, running in. "Look

what he did!" He held up a compact disc that was broken in two pieces. "This was my new Hammer CD!"

"Keep your voice down," Tasha warned. "Daddy's going to come in here."

"Where is he?" Troy lifted the blanket and looked under the bed.

George scooted out of the room and ran down the hall. Tasha and I followed. Troy cornered George in the living room.

"Don't hurt him, Troy," I said. "I'll lend you my Hammer CD and you can tape it, okay?"

Troy wrestled with George for a few more moments, then he looked up. "Okay. Thanks, Laney. Mom would get mad if I killed him anyway."

"There's fudge-swirl ice cream in the freezer," Tasha said as though she had just remembered.

We all tiptoed into the kitchen. Tasha took out the ice cream while Troy got the bowls and spoons. We were all sitting around the table whispering to each other and laughing. By the time we got back in Tasha's room, the two of us were actually speaking!

"Remember the time when you spent the night," Tasha said, "and we tried to bake cupcakes?"

I laughed. "Didn't George break a lamp with one of them?"

We were both sitting on her bed like old times. Then we were silent. "Why were we so mad at each other?" I asked finally.

"I don't know."

"No, really. What happened?"

She shrugged. "I guess I'm just sick of everything coming so easy for you."

I didn't know what to say. I guess to her, everything did look as if it came easy for me. She didn't know how hard I'd worked.

"I'm not jealous of you," she went on. "I just wish you wouldn't go around bragging so much."

"When do I brag?"

"Come off it, Delaney. You always want the spotlight on you."

"The spotlight? You're the one who's always in the spotlight. Look at you! When I'm with you, I might as well be invisible. You're so pretty. And you're the one who's developing, not me."

"Pretty isn't everything." Tasha stood up. "Neither is developing. You don't know what it's like being your friend. Everybody treats you so special. Even my own mother."

I stared at her. Tears were in her eyes, but she tried to keep me from seeing them. "That's not my fault," I said.

"I know, but it still hurts."

I got off the bed and tried to put my arm around her, but she moved away.

"Leave me alone, Delaney."

Quietly I laid the blanket and pillow on the floor and made myself comfortable. Tasha turned off the lights and climbed into bed.

In the darkness I asked, "Why can't we just be friends again?" But she didn't answer me.

5

. . . .

"Today's the big day!" Lauren exclaimed, sticking her head in our dressing room. "Kathleen, you're due in makeup now."

"Are you sure I need makeup?" she asked, admiring herself in the mirror. "I mean, why tamper with perfection?"

Lauren laughed. "Get going, will you?" Kathleen sauntered through the door. "That girl is something else," Lauren said to me.

I didn't say anything.

"What's wrong, Delaney? Aren't you excited about our first promo?"

"I *am* excited," I said.

"Well, let's see some smiling. This show is supposed to be fun."

I tried to smile, which is pretty hard to do when you're not in the mood.

She came into the room and sat with me on the love

seat. "Come on. What's bothering you? We can't have that droopy face in our commercial."

She put her arm around me and I leaned against her. "How come Kathleen got the speaking part and I didn't?"

"Ms. Seachman and I decided on Kathleen because she's the oldest and we figured she could handle the pressure better."

"Because she's the oldest or because she's the prettiest?"

"Who says she's the prettiest?"

I sighed. "That's obvious. She's beautiful."

Lauren looked me in the eye. "What are you talking about? You're just as beautiful as Kathleen. Inside *and* out. Now go get your clothes from wardrobe. Then join Kathleen in makeup."

I stood up and looked into the mirror. "Do you really think I need makeup?" I asked, imitating Kathleen. "Should we risk tampering with the face of Diana Sutherland's daughter?"

"What am I going to do with you?"

Speaking about Diana Sutherland was a regular thing with Kathleen. She loved keeping us up-to-date on her mother's whereabouts. So far she'd been filming a movie in Italy, vacationing on the French Riviera, and making public appearances in London.

I went down the hall to the wardrobe room.

Penny gave Cory a pair of jeans and a red T-shirt. "You can wear your own sneakers," she told him. "Now get to the makeup room."

Cory made a face. "Makeup?"

"Yes, makeup," I teased. "You'd look lovely with a little eye shadow."

"No way, man. I'm not wearing any of that girl stuff."

"If you don't wear makeup, you'll look funny on camera. You know that!"

"I know it. I just don't want to believe it." He left the wardrobe room shaking his head.

Penny handed me a denim skirt and a purple top with a butterfly embroidered on the front. It was beautiful.

When we were all dressed and caked with makeup, we went down to the underground garage. Lauren spent five minutes talking to a man she called Mike, who was sketching something on a legal pad.

"Who is he?" I asked Cory.

"The director. They're talking about how the cameras will be set up."

"I wish we'd leave already. I'm burning up."

"You can say that again."

So I did. "I wish we'd leave already. I'm burning up."

Cory put his hands around my neck and pretended to choke me.

Lauren clapped her hands together. "Okay, let's get going before we fall behind schedule."

We rode to the shoot in Eric's Mercedes-Benz. The car was brand-new and roomy. Cory whispered to me, "Lauren's boyfriend must be very rich."

Lauren turned around. "He's not rich and mind your own business."

Kathleen laughed. "Cory, you whisper louder than normal people talk."

"Sorry, Lauren," he mumbled.

We were shooting the promo at the Empire State Building, which is over a hundred stories high. All the camera equipment was set up on the eighty-sixth-floor observation deck, where tourists go to look out over the entire island of Manhattan. One section of the deck had been closed off so we could work.

"Do you remember your lines, Kathleen?" Lauren asked.

"Sure." She gave me a sidelong glance. "*I'm* not the baby around here."

I rolled my eyes at her and walked away. There were about ten men working and standing around the equipment. The hair stylist came over and combed my hair. When she was finished, I looked about six years old.

We had to do a lot of waiting while Mike and the camera crew did their work. I was still pretty disappointed at not being chosen to do the speaking part, as if just because I was three years younger than Kathleen, I couldn't say a couple of lines.

"Okay, people," Mike yelled after about twenty minutes of setup. "Let's rehearse once before we begin videotaping." Some of the tourists who were on the observation deck were standing around watching, making me a little bit nervous. "Take your places, kids."

Cory climbed a couple of feet up the tall fence.

"Be careful," Lauren said from her position behind the cameras. "That's high enough."

I rested against a big telescope and Kathleen stood by the fence in front of the camera.

One of Mike's assistants took a light reading to make sure there was enough natural light. Then Mike called for action.

Kathleen smiled. "There's a brand-new show starting this fall called 'Friday Afternoon' and . . . and, I forgot my lines!" She started laughing and covering her mouth with her hand. "Okay, okay, I remember now.

There's a brand-new show starting this fall called 'Saturday After—' "

"It's *Friday* Afternoon'!" Cory shouted from the fence. "Get with it, Kathleen. It's not easy hanging here while you blow all your lines."

Kathleen was too busy laughing to hear him so I walked over to her. "This is what you say. 'There's a brand-new show starting this fall called 'Friday Afternoon,' and we have all the stories you want to hear.' "

Cory jumped off the fence. "You're wrong, Laney. It goes, 'We have all the stories you want to *see*.' "

"Hear! See! What difference does it make?" I asked.

Kathleen said, "Yeah, everyone knows what we mean."

Lauren was laughing, too, but she wasn't helping us with the lines.

Cory pushed both Kathleen and me out of the way. "Just watch 'Friday Afternoon,' " he said into the camera and made a funny face. "That's all you have to say!"

Lauren started clapping. "That was great! Let's all go have lunch together."

Behind her the camera crew began taking down the equipment.

We all stared at her. "What do you mean?" Kathleen asked. "We haven't taped the promo yet. We just rehearsed it."

Mike patted her shoulder. "Oh, yes we have. I was videotaping what you three just did."

"Why?" I asked.

"Because it's funny," Lauren said. "You've seen those blooper shows where the actors mess up their lines and start laughing. Well, that's what we're going to use for your promo commercial."

"We'll look stupid," Cory said.

"No, you won't. It will show your audience that you guys are just normal kids. I think they'll get a kick out of seeing you all argue over the lines."

"How did you know we would argue?" I asked.

"I work with you three for seven hours a day. I knew exactly what you would do."

"You're getting sneaky," I told her.

She winked at me. "You have to be a little sneaky in this business."

· · · · · · ·

When we got back to the studio, we went right into the rehearsal room and Mike rolled in a television set so we could see the commercial. "We're going to have to edit it a little," he told us, "but basically we're going to let it air as is."

He popped the videotape in the VCR. Kathleen's face filled up the whole screen at first and she looked very pleasant as she began to introduce the show. Then the look of horror overcame her when she realized she had forgotten her line. By the end of the tape the scene was total chaos. In a weird way it was pretty funny with the three of us all fighting to be in front of the camera.

"Okay, kids," Lauren said. "I want you to get out of these clothes. Then go down the hall and have Meg teach you how to remove the makeup."

"I already know how," Kathleen said. "I'm starting high school this fall."

"Pardon me, my dear," Lauren said, bowing before her as if she were a queen. "I didn't realize I was in the presence of such greatness."

Kathleen tossed her hair and left the room.

I folded my arms across my chest. "Why do you treat her like that, Lauren? You make her think she's so special all the time."

"I don't take her seriously."

"If you had to share a dressing room with her, you'd realize how sickening she is."

"Rise above it, Delaney," Lauren said.

· · · · · · ·

Back in the dressing room with my makeup off and my clothes returned to the wardrobe room, I sat in my official network bathrobe waiting for Kathleen to get out of the shower. She had been in there for forty minutes, and yes, I was counting. I thought of what Lauren had said and decided that I would be the mature one and not get angry.

"It's all yours," she said, finally coming out. Total time: fifty-five minutes.

"Thanks. Glad to see you didn't rush on my account."

"Be quiet, troll." She sat down on the sofa. "You should be glad I let you use my shower at all."

"*Your* shower? It's *our* shower. And *our* dressing room. Unfortunately." I opened the bathroom door.

"I guess you don't know the real reason they put the two of us in here together. They do have other dressing rooms, you know."

I couldn't rise above that one. "What real reason?"

She began moisturizing her legs slowly. She was going to make me wait.

"What real reason?" I repeated.

"Okay, okay. It just so happens that on the first day

Lauren and I had a private talk before you arrived. She asked me if I wouldn't mind sharing with you because she needed someone to look after you. She said you were too young to be in a room all by yourself."

I carefully controlled my voice. "She said that?"

"In other words, she asked me to baby-sit for you while we're in here."

"Liar!" I said, and closed the door behind me.

After my shower we had an hour and a half before I had to go downstairs and wait for Mom to pick me up. So while Kathleen and Cory sat in the hallway eating sunflower seeds, I went down to Lauren's office.

"What can I do for you, Delaney?" Lauren asked. "Did you and Kathleen get into another fight?"

"No, not exactly." I took a seat on the sofa wondering if I should just blurt it out and risk sounding like a whiny tattletale. "Kathleen said the reason we share a dressing room is because you said I need a baby-sitter."

Lauren shook her head. "Perhaps Kathleen misunderstood what I said. I don't think you need a baby-sitter. However, I did ask Kathleen to sort of make sure you were okay. I can't be in a hundred places at once. I asked her to be like a big sister to you."

I stood up and shrugged. "That's all I wanted to know."

"You're overreacting, don't you think?"

"No. I'm finally getting the picture. I'm always going to be the youngest around here, and I guess I just have to deal with it, right?"

I left the office half expecting Lauren to come after me and tell me that she didn't think I was a baby. But she didn't.

• • • • • • •

"I don't have time for breakfast, Mom," I said that Friday. "I want to run up the block and say good-bye to Kelly."

Mom was in the kitchen in her underwear, ironing her dress. "I don't want you going to work on an empty stomach. Why can't you say good-bye to her when you get home this afternoon?"

"She's leaving for camp at noon." I sat on the living room sofa and laced up my sneakers in a hurry. It was eight-twenty. Mom and I had to be in a taxi by eight-forty-five, since I had to be at work at nine.

"Well, come drink a glass of milk. You need your protein." Mom is hung up on protein.

By the time I arrived at Kelly's house, it was eight-thirty. Kelly was sitting on the living room floor packing up her trunk. "Where's my canteen?" she yelled to her mother as I took a seat next to her.

"It's in my bedroom, honey. Don't wake the baby."

"I'll be right back, Laney. I don't want to forget anything."

When she left, I looked at all the stuff she was going to take to camp. New shorts, T-shirts, and sandals. She even had a new bathing suit. Pink, of course.

I felt left out. I really wanted to go even though I knew it was impossible.

Kelly came back into the living room giggling. "Look what my mother bought for me."

She handed me a small plastic package. Inside was a pink training bra with a little white bow in the front. "Isn't that funny?" Kelly asked. "She thinks I might start grow-ing at camp."

"It's possible."

Kelly put the package inside her trunk and continued packing. "It's going to feel weird without you. I hope our friendship can last a whole month apart."

I hadn't thought about that. We could do a lot of chang-ing in a month. Then I noticed that she was still wearing her friendship bracelet. So was I. Holding up my wrist, I said, "I think our friendship can survive another month. Don't you?"

She gave me a tiny smile. "Of course."

The clock read eight-fifty. "I'm going to be late!" We hugged. "Have fun."

"I'll write you as often as I can," she said. "I'll miss you."

"I'll miss you, too." I headed for the front door. "Bye."

· · · · · · ·

I was five minutes late for work. Running out of the el-evator, I made it to the rehearsal room in three seconds flat. I opened the door and was met by a very angry stare from Lauren. "Ms. Seachman would like to see you in her office right now," she said.

My mouth hung open. "Huh?"

Both Kathleen and Cory were staring at me, too. I was totally embarrassed.

"Get going, Delaney."

I left the room and headed slowly toward Ms. Seach-man's office. The secretary told me to go right in; Ms. Seachman was expecting me.

Ms. Seachman looked up from her work as I walked in. "Delaney, have a seat."

I wasn't sure if she meant on one of the sofas or at her desk, so I sat on a sofa because it was farther away from her. Then I waited and waited while she continued writing. After about fifteen minutes I was convinced she had forgotten I was there, so I cleared my throat slightly.

It didn't work. She continued to work, made a phone call to someone named Paul about a luncheon she was attending that afternoon, and buzzed her secretary to ask her about some meeting the producers were having.

I squirmed and fidgeted like crazy. The waiting was bad, but not knowing what she'd do to me was worse.

Then finally she dropped her pen and spoke to me. "Miss Crawford, are you aware that you are to be here at nine A.M. sharp?"

"Yes. I'm sorry I was late. It's just—"

"I'm not interested in hearing your excuse. We are on a tight schedule this summer and I will not tolerate you waltzing in here any time you please. It's only the third week of preproduction, so maybe now is the time to remind you that you can be easily replaced. Do you understand?"

"Yes, Ms. Seachman. It won't happen again."

"I know," she said. "You may leave now."

I tiptoed out and walked quickly back to the rehearsal room. Ms. Seachman is one tough lady. But I guess it's like Mom says. When you're a woman in charge, sometimes you have to go out of your way to show people you mean business. One thing was for sure. I would never be late again.

6

. . . .

I worked in Mom's office on Saturday answering the telephone since her receptionist had the weekend off. On our lunch hour Mom and I went uptown to a museum that displayed paintings and sculpture by African and Caribbean artists. Every time there is a new exhibit we rush over to see it.

On the way back we stopped off at a health food restaurant and ordered takeout. When we got back to the dental office Dr. Cahill's son, Bryce, was standing in the hallway begging his father for money. I didn't really know him that well, but something told me I'd be seeing a lot more of him now that Mom and Dr. Cahill were dating.

"I gave you your allowance already," Dr. Cahill said firmly. "If you want more, you're going to have to work for it."

"Work?" Bryce sounded as if it was the first time he had heard the word.

"Yes, work. When I was fourteen I had a summer job. Why don't you try to find something like that?"

Mom and I left the two of them in the hallway and went into her office. There was a red rose on her desk and a little envelope with Mom's name on it. She opened the envelope, read the card, and smiled.

I wanted her to share the card with me, but she put it back in the envelope without saying anything. While we ate I was dying to know what it said, so later, while Mom was with a patient, I sneaked a peek.

Lisa,
    I saw this perfect rose and thought of you.
Love, Josh

Love? They couldn't already be in love, could they?

When Mom came back into her office, I was daydreaming, looking out the window.

"Why don't you and Bryce go for a walk?" she asked. "It's a nice day out."

"I don't feel like it. I wish Kelly were home."

Mom came over and sat on the end of the desk. "I'm sorry that you couldn't go to camp with your friends, Delaney. But remember, you gave it up for something you really want to do."

I nodded. What she was saying was true. Deep down I was glad I had decided to take the job, even if it wasn't much fun yet. After all, camp would always be there, but "Friday Afternoon" was a once-in-a-lifetime opportunity.

· · · · · · ·

Without Kelly the weekend was so long and boring that I actually looked forward to another workweek. On Monday morning as I stepped off the elevator, I was greeted by a stream of water directly in my face.

Cory laughed. "Gotcha, Laney!" He twirled a water gun around his finger and took off down the hallway.

I dropped my knapsack by the watercooler and chased him all the way to our dressing rooms. Water dripped from my face and hair onto my T-shirt. "I'm going to kill you, Cory," I screamed.

He stopped running just long enough to squirt me again. Then he ducked into his dressing room. "I'm safe," he declared coolly. "Remember the rules."

That's what he thought. I slipped into his dressing room and grabbed the gun from his hand. "Take this!" I squirted it at him until it was empty.

Then as I turned to leave, guess who was standing in the doorway. "What do you two think you're doing?" Ms. Seachman demanded with her hands on her hips. Cory and I looked at each other. Neither of us knew what to say. Especially me. After all I was the one in Cory's dressing room holding the water gun.

"Miss Crawford. Mr. Drennen. I want to see you both in my office in five minutes. Do you think you can follow that simple request?"

We were both so scared we could only nod.

"Good." She continued down the hallway. I turned to Cory. "Suppose she gives me the ax this time?"

"I'm the one who's going to get in trouble. I brought the stupid water gun."

"But I shouldn't have come in here. I knew the rules."

I gave him back the gun. "Now I'm going to lose my job before we even got started."

I walked out of his dressing room and went down the hall for my knapsack. Then I walked back toward Ms. Seachman's office very slowly. It started to hit me then. This could be the end of the line for me.

Cory was waiting for me outside Ms. Seachman's office. Without saying a word, we went inside together.

"Please close the door behind you," Ms. Seachman said. She was seated at her desk with tons of paper in front of her.

I pushed the door shut, then took a seat next to Cory on the sofa. The only difference between this time and the last was that Ms. Seachman let us have it right away. "Is there a reason the two of you are dripping wet first thing in the morning?"

Cory lowered his head. "I brought a water gun with me. I just wanted to have some fun."

"This is not the place for fun, young man. We have a lot of work to do in a short amount of time." She faced me. "Is this going to be an everyday thing with you, Delaney? Am I going to have to take time out of my daily schedule to discipline you?"

"No," I said, fidgeting nervously. "It was an accident. I knew I wasn't supposed to go into his dressing room. I just didn't think."

Ms. Seachman stared at both of us. "Was I wrong to think you could behave yourselves without constant supervision?"

Cory and I mumbled, "No," together.

"Do I need to hire someone to watch over you kids?"

Again we said, "No."

"I don't want to have this discussion with either of you again. You have five minutes to get to rehearsal room."

Cory and I rose from the sofa and headed for the door. Cory was the first one out, but before I could leave Ms. Seachman called me back.

"Yes?" I said, turning toward her. I could sense what was going to happen next. She was going to fire me.

Ms. Seachman stood up and walked closer to me. Her eyes burned holes in my skin. She seemed to be trying to figure out if I was worth the hassle. "This is the second time I've had to talk to you. The last thing I need around here is a troublemaker."

"It won't happen again," I said quickly, almost begging. "I promise this time."

"It had better not. You know what they say. Three strikes and you're out."

She dismissed me, and I ran to the rehearsal room. Kathleen and Cory were already there, seated on the floor. I joined them. Cory and I exchanged secret glances at one another. Kathleen was the last person we wanted to find out about what happened to us.

"Welcome to the fourth week of preproduction," Lauren said, coming through the door. Then she sat with us on the floor and told us about one of the show's features. The segment involved one of us going into the street and asking kids a different question each week. "It's called 'Listen Up!' " she said. "And it's a way for kids to say what's on their minds."

It sounded like a pretty neat idea. I could see myself

on the street holding a microphone and picking kids to answer my question for the cameras.

"Kathleen, this will be one of your jobs."

I looked up surprised. Why her?

Kathleen smiled. "Terrific."

My cheeks burned with envy. It looked like what Kathleen had said was true. She *was* the star of the show.

· · · · · · ·

I received my first letter from Kelly that Friday. I tore it open excitedly.

Dear Laney,

How are you? I'm having a good time, but I wish you were here. I hope you aren't working too hard. And I hope you aren't bored.

Tasha and I are bunkies. She's on the bottom and I got stuck with the top. We don't talk to each other unless it's necessary. I keep thinking about how mean she treated you.

Oh, well. Most of the girls in our cabin are back from last year, but there are two new girls. One girl is from Hawaii! I wish you could meet her because she's so pretty and interesting.

The older girls in cabin 4-B are just as stuck-up as ever. They all wear bikinis and they think they are so hot. We have to get back at them for what they did last year.

Oh, no! I have to go now. Quiet time is over and we are going to play tennis and volleyball. I miss you.

Kelly O.

A little while later Mom came into the kitchen, all dressed up in a black cocktail dress and her good pearls. "Do I look all right?"

"You look great. Is that a new dress?"

"I bought it this afternoon on my lunch break. Honestly, if I charge another thing on that credit card they're going to come and arrest me."

"Did you buy anything for me?"

"Was I supposed to?"

"You always buy something for me when you run up your charge card."

She smiled. "You know me too well. Go look in my bedroom."

In one of the shopping bags on her bed there was a box of beautiful peach-colored stationery with a lacy border. I couldn't wait to write Kelly back.

Dear Kelly,

I miss you, too. And I'm real, real, REAL bored without you. But I'm glad you are having fun. Too bad you got stuck being bunkies with Tasha. If I were you I would watch my back.

I'm working real hard on the show, and I got in BIGGG trouble the day I came to say good-bye to you because I was late for work. I thought I was going to get fired, but I didn't.

I'm sure Tasha is telling you all kinds of lies about me. Don't believe a word she says. You know me better than she does anyway. And please stay on my side.

Delaney C.

· · · · · · ·

It was about nine o'clock on Saturday, and I was already dressed because Mom had to go into the office for a few hours. And of course I had to go, too.

"Hurry up," Mom said. I was unloading the dishwasher. "You'll have to finish that when we get back."

Rush, rush, rush. Her first patient wasn't until ten.

Then the doorbell rang, surprising both of us. Mom opened the door and laughed. It was her best friend, Neema. She and her husband had spent the last few months in Egypt doing research for a college textbook they were writing.

Mom and Neema hugged like crazy. "When did you get back?" Mom asked.

"Last night. I was going to call, but it was after midnight."

"Gosh, you look terrific."

Neema was dressed in a long, colorful African dress and head wrap. Even her accent had changed.

"How's my favorite little girl?" she asked me, giving me a big hug and kiss. I didn't get her usual "my, how you've grown" speech, because we both know I haven't grown an inch since she last saw me.

"Great," I said, and told her all about my new job.

Then Mom said, "I can't wait to hear about your trip, Neema, but right now we're on our way to my office."

The doorbell rang again. This time it was Dr. Cahill. "I was in the neighborhood and wondered if you two wanted a lift to the office."

He leaned over to give Mom a kiss on the lips, but she moved her head so it landed on her cheek instead. "Joshua, you remember my friend Neema Shaw, don't you?" Mom asked nervously.

"Yes, yes." They shook hands. "It's nice to see you again."

"Same here," Neema said, but she was looking at Mom.

Mom led Dr. Cahill back out the door. "Joshua, maybe you'd better go ahead without me and get the air conditioner going. We'll walk over."

When he had left, Neema continued staring at Mom with one eyebrow raised. "There's something going on between the two of you, isn't there?"

"What makes you think that?"

"I'm not blind."

"Neema, please don't start." Mom grabbed her pocketbook. "You don't know anything about it."

"Lisa, I can't believe you. What kind of example are you setting for Delaney?"

Mom glanced at me and I looked down, pretending not to be listening. "Neema," she said in one of her strong whispers. "I don't want to discuss my personal life with you if you're going to have that attitude. Come on, Delaney."

The three of us left the apartment and walked down the stairs to the front door. I didn't like seeing them angry at each other, but I guess all friends have arguments, not just Tasha and me.

"Lisa, why don't you let me spend the day with Delaney? There's no sense in her spending a beautiful day like this cooped up in a stuffy office."

"Yeah, Mom."

Mom hesitated.

Neema said, "Come on. I have a whole bunch of pictures from my trip and some beautiful African artwork and jewelry I picked up. We can go to the park, and I can tell her all about Egypt."

"Please, Mom."

Mom didn't look happy, but she gave me a hug and whispered that she loved me. Then when we were across the street she called out, "Have fun."

· · · · · · · ·

By the time I got home that afternoon, I was very confused. Neema and I had spent about four hours together and all she kept talking about was Mom and Dr. Cahill. She'd asked me a zillion questions about them.

"Is that you, honey?" Mom asked from the den.

"Yeah. Who else has a key?" I opened the freezer, found a broken ice cube, and popped it in my mouth.

Then I went into the den and started playing one of my video games. After a while Mom put down her paperwork and joined me on the floor. "Teach me how to play this thing."

"I don't feel like it."

"Did Neema upset you?"

"No, not really."

"What's wrong, then?"

I took a deep breath. "Have you forgotten about Dad?"

Mom looked surprised. She ran her hand down my cheek. "My goodness. Of course not. Did Neema—"

"Neema has nothing to do with it." For some reason tears began to roll down my face. "It's just . . . Do you think Dad would want you to date Dr. Cahill?"

She shrugged. "I don't know. I suppose your father would want me to be happy again." She put her arm around me and drew me closer to her. "And Joshua makes me very happy."

I sobbed on her shoulder. "Neema said it's wrong for you to date him. She said dating someone white will deny me my culture."

Mom kissed me. "Neema and I are old friends, but we have different opinions on a lot of things. My relationship with Joshua will have no effect on your culture. I'm very proud to be African-American and I want you to be, too."

"I am."

"Well, suppose I told you not to be friends with Kelly anymore. How would that make you feel?"

"She's my best friend in the whole world."

"Do you see what I'm trying to say? I've always given you the freedom to choose your friends, and you choose both black and white friends. Now you have to allow me the freedom to choose my friends." She held me for a few more minutes. "Does that sound fair?"

I nodded.

"Good. Now are you going to teach me how to play this thing or not? It cost me an arm and a leg, you know."

I wiped my eyes. "Okay, okay, but you can't give up this time."

· · · · · · ·

Mom and I cooked dinner together that night. Steamed asparagus, potato pancakes, and homemade applesauce. Then we set the places at the counter, using the good china that Mom and Dad had received when they got married.

I loved it when it was just Mom and me doing things together without interruption. It was a special time.

While Mom carefully washed the delicate dishes, I dried. "Can we have a lot more evenings like this?" I asked.

"We sure can."

"What about all the time you spend with Dr. Cahill?"

She handed me the last fork. "You always come first, Delaney. You know that."

I smiled. Sometimes I just needed to be reminded.

· · · · · · ·

Finally another letter from Kelly arrived.

Dear Laney,

I'm still having a good time and I still wish you were here. Tasha and I have been spending a lot of time learning to ride horses. It's kind of fun once you get over being afraid.

How's work? I hope you haven't gotten in any more trouble. I feel guilty for making you late that day.

Right now Tasha is putting my hair in a French braid. We're going swimming as soon as quiet time is over. Don't worry, she promised not to look over my shoulder and read this letter, so it's still private.

Tasha is not all that bad. In fact, we have a lot in common. But she doesn't know how to tell people how she feels, that's all. And I think she's a little jealous of you.

Maybe when we get back we can all be best friends together. Wouldn't that be nice?

See you soon!

Kelly O.

I ripped the pages in half, then in quarters, then in eighths. When I tried for sixteenths I wasn't strong enough, so I threw the whole stack across the den.

Tasha had a lot of nerve. Just because I wasn't there, she was trying to take my place with Kelly.

I grabbed a sheet of stationery. Someone had to warn Kelly.

Dear Kelly,

I just finished reading your letter. Are you crazy? Have you forgotten how Tasha has been acting lately? She's just using you. I'm sure of it! She never wanted to be your friend before. She only hung out with you because of me.

And now all she wants to do is hurt me. Can't you see that? Come on, Kelly. Open your eyes!

Your only true best friend,
Delaney C.

P.S. I don't care if you let Tasha read this.

7

. . . .

"I hate makeup," Cory mumbled as we walked down the hallway toward the studio. We were all dressed and made-up because we were taking publicity photos.

"Hurry up, you guys," Lauren said, standing in the doorway. "Time is money." She held the door for us.

Actually, it was the first time we had been in the studio. It wasn't very large, but it had three beautiful sets. On the left side of the room there was a news desk with a sign behind it that read BITS & PIECES.

In the middle of the room there were three director-style chairs in front of twelve video screens. Each chair had one of our names on it.

And on the right side of the room there was a miniature staircase with only three steps. Above the staircase was another sign. This one read FRIDAY AFTERNOON in fancy lettering with bright colors.

"What do you think?" Lauren asked us.

We all nodded our approval. For the first time it felt as if we were doing a real show.

"Kids, go sit on the stairs for the first set of photographs. This is where you'll be doing most of the show."

We took our seats, each on a different step. Kathleen was on top, then Cory, then me. A couple of minutes later a photographer came into the studio and began snapping pictures. He made us switch places twice so he could get us in different positions.

Next we moved to the directors' chairs. They were so high off the ground I could hardly get into mine. Kathleen laughed. "Lauren, we're going to need a stepladder over here for the little one."

The photographer took about another thirty pictures on that set. Kathleen kept fluffing her hair in between shots and asking the photographer if he was capturing her glow and radiance.

Finally he stopped and we all headed over to the news set, but there was only one chair.

"Go have a seat, Cory," Lauren said. "You're going to be our anchorman."

"Me?" He settled in behind the desk.

I looked up at Lauren. "How come I'm not the news anchor?"

"Ms. Seachman picked Cory."

"Don't be a baby," Kathleen teased.

That was easy for her to say. She already had an assignment.

• • • • • • •

"The sitter will be here in a few minutes," Mom said that evening, standing in the bathroom putting on lipstick. "I don't want you watching TV all night. You should be in bed by nine."

I leaned against the doorframe. "I don't see why you have to go out with him on a weeknight."

"We're not going on a date. We're just going to one of those protect-the-environment meetings. I'll be back around ten."

I'd already be asleep by then. "But I wanted to talk to you about what's going on at work."

"Is Lauren giving you a hard time? You weren't late again, were you?"

I shook my head. "No, I was a half hour early. It's just that, well—"

The doorbell rang. Mom looked at me. "Maybe we can talk about it over breakfast tomorrow, okay?" She kissed my forehead. "I'm sorry." Then she rushed off to answer the door.

Something told me she'd be busy tomorrow, too.

• • • • • • •

I was right. Mom was too busy to talk during breakfast. Well, to talk to *me*, anyway. She spent a half hour on the phone with Dr. Cahill. "You did look a little pale last night," she said to him sympathetically. "I'll have Jill cancel all your appointments, okay?"

I stared into my apple juice.

"Sure, Joshua. I'd be glad to see Maria. And I'll try to check up on you at lunchtime. Can I bring you anything?"

I wanted to throw up.

Mom laughed. "Okay then. I'll be by at noon to feed you soup."

When she hung up, she apologized. "I didn't think that

phone call would take so long, but Joshua isn't coming in to the office today. He thinks it's the flu."

"So he's got you taking over his patients?" I knew my tone was angry, but I couldn't help it.

"Only one. She needs her teeth done before she goes to college."

"I can't even remember the last time you stayed home sick."

"I'm just naturally healthy," she joked. "Come on, don't be mad. What did you want to talk to me about?"

"Forget it," I said, and got up from the table. "You have soup to make."

· · · · · · ·

Since I was a little early that morning, I spent a few minutes admiring the ivory giraffe in the lobby of the network building. There was so much detail carved into it that it must have taken years to complete. It reminded me of the giraffe in the photograph on my bedroom wall.

Cory came up behind me. "You really like this thing, right?"

I nodded. I wasn't in the mood to talk.

"What's wrong?" he asked. "I hope you're not still upset about being left out of the news job. I don't know why they picked me over you. You have the most experience with cameras, and you're a much better speaker than I am. Remember, I'm the one with the famous New Jersey accent."

I smiled. "No, it's not you. It's the show. I guess I won't have anything special to do, that's all."

He put his arm around my shoulder and we walked together toward the elevator. Neither of us said anything, but I was beginning to think I should have ditched this stupid show and gone to camp.

· · · · · · ·

"We have a busy day," Lauren told us at our meeting in the rehearsal room. "So let me give you the bad news first. I've cancelled your speech class today. We'll be spending most of the day in the studio. Kathleen and Cory, I want you two to go into the studio now and familiarize yourselves with the sets. Delaney, wait here. I'll be right back."

Everyone left, and I sat on the floor wondering why I was being singled out. I couldn't be in trouble again. Five minutes later Lauren came back with a woman I had never seen before.

I stood up, nervously.

"Delaney, this is Fran, our excellent caterer. She needs to talk to you for a few minutes. After you finish, I want you to come into the studio and work with Mike."

When Lauren left, Fran said, "Ms. Seachman tells me you're on a restricted diet, and since I'm going to be providing the food on the set, I need to find out what you can eat and what you can't."

"I eat everything except meat."

"Chicken, fish?" she asked.

I shook my head. "No."

"Milk products, cheese, eggs?"

"They're okay."

"What about beverages?"

"Natural juices, spring water, and milk. I don't drink soda or anything."

"What about sugar?"

I smiled. "My mother would probably tell you only once in a while, but I like to cheat every now and then."

"Maybe we'd better listen to your mother."

"Why did I open my big mouth?" I asked more to myself than to Fran.

She laughed. "Okay then, there shouldn't be a problem. Starting next Friday I'll be sending over all the meals for the cast and crew. I'll put your food on a separate platter with a sticker on it with your name."

· · · · · · ·

After that meeting I went down to the studio. Lauren was at the news desk working with Cory and two cameramen. "I'm here," I told Lauren.

She nodded. "Okay. Go take a seat until Mike gets here."

"What are you doing?"

"I'm showing Cory how to work with the cameras."

"Can I watch?"

"Delaney, you're interrupting us. Please take a seat and wait for Mike."

"Fine," I said, and walked over to the "Friday Afternoon" set. On the other side of the room Kathleen was holding a microphone and practicing for her Listen Up! segment with one of the associate producers.

A good five minutes went by. I stood up and walked around the room, trying to get close enough to hear what Lauren was saying, but far enough away so she wouldn't notice me. Slowly I inched closer and closer until . . .

"Delaney, would you please go have a seat. Mike should be down from the control room any minute."

"But I'm bored."

"If you want to be an actress, you'd better get used to waiting." She had the same kind of look on her face that Mom sometimes gets with me. The one that means she's holding back her temper.

Everyone was staring at me now. "I'm not doing anything. I'm just standing here."

She shook her head and said to one of the cameramen, "I'm never having children. Honestly."

He laughed.

That did it. "Oh, so I'm the child here, right? The eleven-year-old who doesn't know how to do anything." My voice was rising. "Well, how are you supposed to know what I can do if you never assign me anything?"

She pointed toward the door. "Delaney, turn around right now and go to my office. I don't want to hear another word from you."

"Fine. I have nothing more to say."

· · · · · · ·

I paced up and down Lauren's office furiously. This time I didn't care if I got fired because I had just about had it with "Friday Afternoon" and Lauren, and Ms. Seachman, and Kathleen.

Lauren rushed into the office, slammed the door behind her, and threw her clipboard down on her desk angrily. "Just who do you think you are? Are you some hotshot celebrity who should be treated differently than everybody else?"

I wasn't about to be intimidated. "I don't want to be treated differently," I said louder than usual. "I want to be treated fairly."

We were standing just a few feet from one another, and

for a second she just stared at me. "And how have you been treated unfairly?"

"Come on, Lauren. Everybody else has something special to do on the show except me."

She ran her fingers through her hair and plunked herself in her chair. Then she took a long, deep breath. "And how do you know you won't be given something special to do?"

I folded my arms.

"Delaney, this isn't the place for jealousy and selfishness. We're a team, which means we're supposed to work together as one. Every member of our team serves a different purpose, and every purpose is equally important."

"But I don't have a purpose!"

"You *do* have a purpose. I just haven't gotten around to handing out all the assignments yet. Will you be patient and allow me to do my job?"

I nodded.

"You know, Delaney, I'm beginning to think I was wrong about you. When we first met at the interview, I saw your videotape and I saw how much you are capable of. I thought the others could benefit from your experience. I thought you would be the one to help the others, but instead you've become the problem."

Her words hurt me inside. I let out a slow breath, the way we learned in speech class. "I'm sorry, Lauren. Really."

"Aren't you getting tired of apologizing for your behavior?"

"But I mean it this time. If you still want to work with me, I'll cooperate."

"I'm going to hold you to that." She stood up. "Stay

here for ten minutes and get yourself together, then come back to the studio with a smile on your face, full of apologies. And we're going to forget about all of this."

"What about Ms. Seachman? She told me three strikes and I'm out."

"She doesn't know about this. If you don't cause any more trouble today, there's no reason she'll have to find out."

"Thanks. And I mean it. No more jealousy."

After she left, I took a seat and waited for the ten minutes to go by. She was right. I was the problem. Apologies didn't mean anything by themselves. It was time to improve and become responsible. This was my job.

By the time I left her office, I was determined to make a drastic change. I would do what I was told to do, and I wouldn't whine anymore about how unfairly I was being treated. As she said, I would smile, apologize, and forget all about this.

8

A week later the countdown began.

"Five more rehearsal days left," Lauren said, walking around the rehearsal room like a dictator. "Then you're going before the cameras, ready or not."

Her words scared me. It didn't seem as if we knew what we were doing yet, and I couldn't see how one week could make that much of a difference.

"Today at ten o'clock we're going across the hall to watch the taping of 'The Business Review' show. Then at eleven we're going upstairs to sit in the audience of 'The International Chef.' "

Cory groaned. "Do we have to?"

"Yes, we have to. I want you guys to see some actual shows being taped."

"Sounds like fun," Kathleen said sarcastically.

Actually, it wasn't bad. True, those shows were pretty dull. I wondered who actually watched them and liked them. I mean I like cooking and all, but watching someone chop mushrooms is not my idea of a good time.

At eleven-thirty I went back to my dressing room to get my money. Kathleen was in front of the mirror fixing her hair. I'm surprised she hasn't combed herself bald by now.

"I'm thinking about going blond," she said. "What do you think?"

"I think you're sitting at my makeup table."

She stood up. "Here. You need it more than I do."

There was a knock on the door. "Kathleen, are you ready?" Cory asked through the door. They were going to McDonald's together.

After they had gone, I grabbed my knapsack, went out into the hallway, and bumped into Lauren. Literally. "Delaney, great. You haven't gone yet. Let's go have lunch together."

"Just you and me?" I was smiling.

"Yeah. A business lunch. Come on."

Twenty minutes later we were eating at an Italian restaurant on Forty-fourth Street. She was having the linguini with clam sauce. I was having the pasta primavera. "How are you doing, Delaney?"

Small talk from Lauren? I couldn't believe it. "I'm okay. . . . And you?"

"Just fine. I'm getting a little nervous about the show. This is the first time I've put together a production as big as this, and I just hope it comes off okay."

"It will. You did a good job."

"Oh, Delaney, I wasn't fishing for a compliment. The purpose of this power lunch is to tell you about your special assignment."

"What do I have to do?" I asked excitedly.

She laughed. "Relax, would you? You are the most high-strung child I've ever met."

I sat back trying to restrain my curiosity.

"Every week we'll be doing a segment entitled A Day in the Life of . . . , where we will follow a specific person around from sunup to sundown and find out what an average day is like for him or her."

"Sunup to sundown?"

She nodded. "For the first show we're going to do A Day in the Life of a Figure Skater, and we have Wendy Newman, the junior champion, lined up already. She's your age, and the experts say she'll be a big name in a few years. Probably a gold medalist in the Olympics."

I kept myself completely under control. She hadn't officially offered me the assignment yet.

"Not only will this assignment take up a lot of time, it will also involve doing voice-overs. Have you ever done that before?"

I shook my head.

"After we tape the segment and cut it down to about seven and a half minutes, you'll have to go into a recording booth and explain what's going on to the viewers. Basically all you'll be doing is reading from a script."

"How come you want me to do it and not Kathleen the Great?" As soon as I said it, I knew it sounded awful. "I'm sorry," I said immediately. "I promised I wouldn't be jealous anymore."

Lauren looked impressed. "I'm glad to see you're trying, Delaney. That's very mature of you. The reason I'm giving you this assignment is because you're the best person for it. You're the most comfortable on camera, and I think you can handle the voice-overs with no difficulty."

"Thanks," I said. "I'll do my best."

"Well, that's all we can ask."

I took a sip of water and felt good for the first time in weeks. Lauren *did* have confidence in me. She didn't think I was just a baby.

"How's everything at home?" she asked after a while.

"Okay." There was no reason to tell her about Mom and Dr. Cahill and all of that. It wasn't professional to bring personal problems to work.

"I keep thinking about Friday and how upset you were. I discussed it with Eric, and maybe I didn't handle the situation correctly. I shouldn't have gotten angry at you. I should have listened to you."

I couldn't believe *she* was apologizing to *me*.

She put her hand on mine. "Sometimes I forget how young and sensitive you are. I want you to know that if you're having a problem either at home or at work, you can come to me and we'll talk. Okay?"

I nodded. "Okay."

"Good," She smiled at me. "Now eat all your vegetables."

· · · · · · ·

The last day of preproduction came before we knew what was happening. All week I had worked with Lauren and one of the associate producers on my A Day in the Life of . . . segment. It involved me doing short interviews and taking part in the person's daily activities. I was pretty excited about it.

At ten o'clock Ms. Seachman came into the rehearsal

room to explain what it took to be a good interviewer. Lauren had just shown us a video clip of Barbara Walters interviewing Robin Williams, and we had taken notes on it.

"A good interviewer is also a good listener," Ms. Seachman said. "You have to give the subject your full attention at all times. Wouldn't it be embarrassing to ask a question he or she had just answered?"

"Won't we have a list of questions?" Kathleen asked.

"Yes," Lauren answered. "And you will have plenty of time to prepare. The researchers will make up an information packet for you to read several days before the interview. It will contain background information on the person, newspaper clippings, and anything that will help you know more about him or her. It will also have a list of possible questions."

"But don't get locked into those questions," Ms. Seachman cautioned. "For instance, suppose the person you are interviewing mentions a book he's writing, which you didn't know about before. Do you just forget that he mentioned it?"

"No, we should ask him a couple of questions about it," Cory said.

"Right. You have to listen closely and work with the person. No matter who it is." She smiled. "Do you think we should tell them now, Lauren?"

"Tell us what?" I asked. Finally the secret was to be revealed.

"We might as well," Lauren said. "It's too good to keep to ourselves any longer."

"What is it?" Kathleen asked.

Ms. Seachman said, "Guess who we've arranged for you three to interview on your first show?"

"Who?" we all said together.

"Billy Denim."

Kathleen screamed. "Billy Denim!"

I thought I would faint. "*The* Billy Denim? The rock star?"

"The one and only," Lauren said. She was laughing, too.

"He is positively gorgeous," Kathleen gushed. "I can't believe I'm actually going to meet him, be in the same room with him!"

"He's not that cute," Cory said. "But he does play a mean guitar!"

"I love his song 'Taking All I Can Get,' " I said. "The man is a genius."

"A *gorgeous* genius!" Kathleen said.

Ms. Seachman clapped her hands together. "Okay, everyone. Let's remember we're professionals here. We are not going to be very good interviewers if we act like crazy fans. Lauren, I'll be in my office. Have them prepare some questions that they'd like to ask Mr. Denim."

When she was gone, Lauren asked, "Did she just say 'Mr. Denim'?"

We laughed. You couldn't call a rocker like Billy Denim "Mr. Denim."

"But she's right, you know," Lauren said. "We have to be cool when we meet him. Come on, let's get some questions together."

"Maybe we can ask him how he stays so incredibly sexy," Kathleen suggested.

I just couldn't bring myself down to earth quickly enough to start thinking again. In a zillion years I never would have figured on meeting Billy Denim and actually talking to him.

A long moment of silence passed with nobody saying anything. We were daydreaming. Finally Lauren said, "Okay, let's take a ten-minute Billy Denim break and then get back to work. I have to admit I'm just as excited as you are. What will I wear? Do you think my hair looks okay this way?"

Everybody laughed.

Lauren went to her pocketbook and pulled out the newest Billy Denim cassette. She popped it in her portable tape player. The song "One Plus One Equals Love" came on. It was a slow, beautiful ballad. I lay on the floor and closed my eyes, wondering what he would be like in person.

At ten after eleven we finally finished thinking up the list of questions and even rehearsed the order in which we'd ask them. Lauren left the room to have one of the secretaries type up the list and make copies of it for our info packs.

"Can you believe it's the end of summer rehearsals?" Cory asked. "Remember the first day? It seemed like this day would never get here."

"This was the worst summer of my life," Kathleen said. "I've never spent a vacation in the city before."

"Aw, poor little baby," I teased.

Lauren came back into the room before Kathleen could say anything to me.

"You'll have your info packs by noon. In the meantime, let me give you guys your schedules."

This is what mine looked like:

Tuesday September 4th	11:00–3:00	Makeup, wardrobe, travel, tape interview with Billy Denim
Thursday September 6th	5:00–	Makeup, wardrobe, travel, tape A Day in the Life of segment
Saturday September 8th	8:00–6:00	Travel to airport, flight #114 to Rochester, NY, tape throughout the day at Letchworth State Park
Sunday September 9th	10:00–9:00	Tape fossil dig at Fall- brook, flight #210 to New York City
Wednesday September 12th	4:00–6:00	View movie *Class Secrets*

"Is that five o'clock in the morning on Thursday?" I asked Lauren.

"You got it. Sunup to sundown, remember?"

I gasped. "And what time will I be done?"

"You'll be finished when Wendy Newman is finished. But don't worry. You'll have several breaks throughout the day. You'll only be working on camera for a few hours.

"Five o'clock in the morning?" I asked again. I would have to get up at three-thirty in order to get to the studio on time.

We didn't go to lunch that day. Ms. Seachman threw a surprise end-of-preproduction party for the cast and crew.

I had to admit I was getting scared. There was a lot of work I still had to do before next week. I had two info packs to read, one on Billy Denim, the other on Wendy Newman. And I had to practice my questioning techniques so that I would sound natural on camera. My weekend was booked solid.

9

The phone rang early the next morning. When I picked it up, all I heard was "I'm home!" It was Kelly.

I let out an excited scream. "I didn't think you'd be home until tonight."

"My father had to pick me up real early because he and the team are flying out to L.A. this afternoon." Kelly's father is the batting coach for the New York Mets, and during baseball season he's only home when the team is in town.

"So tell me all about camp. Who was in our cabin this year?"

"Everyone. Jan, Melanie, Nancy. Oh, you should *see* Nancy. She lost so much weight. She even helped our cabin win the diving competition. She was terrific."

"Oh, I wish I could have seen her."

"And guess who else was real good. Tasha. She was like a swan this year."

"Oh." I couldn't think of anything else to say.

"I know you and she aren't talking, but she was really nice the whole time. And really fun. You should have seen some of the wild things she thought up. This summer we definitely won the war against the older girls."

I didn't want to hear it.

"One day we snuck into their cabin, stole all their underwear, and hung it in the trees over on the boys' side. Those girls were so embarrassed. You should have seen them."

I wanted to laugh, but I figured that would only make her keep talking. Of course, she kept on anyway.

"And one night Tasha woke us all up and we tiptoed out of our cabin so the counselor wouldn't hear us. Then Tasha told us to fill our canteens with water and we snuck over to the older girls' cabin and we poured water on each of their beds so they would think they had wet the bed. And we didn't get caught. I wish we could have seen their faces when they woke up."

"That's mean," I said.

"Come on, Laney. It was excellent. And they've done worse stuff to us. Don't you remember the honey they put in our sneakers?"

I had to admit that was worse than anything Tasha had come up with. It had taken us hours of scrubbing down by the lake to clean them out and another whole day for the sneakers to dry.

"And then Tasha—"

"Kelly," I interrupted. If she said Tasha's name again I didn't know what I'd do. "I . . . uh, have to get off the phone now. My mother wants to use it." Total lie. "We can talk later."

"Sure. There's so much to tell you. Tasha and I are

going to play jump rope with some girls from Eleventh Street in a little while. Want to come?"

"Okay. I'll be up at your house in a few minutes."

When I hung up, I stepped into the den where Mom was vacuuming. "Can I go on the next block with Kelly and Tasha to play jump rope?"

Mom switched off the vacuum cleaner. "Don't you have a lot of reading to do before the interview on Tuesday?"

"It's not that much. And I have all day tomorrow and Monday to do it." Monday was Labor Day, our first weekday off from work.

"Well, I'm going down to the office at noon. I only have five patients scheduled, so I should be back no later than three o'clock. Have fun with your friends. I know how miserable you were because you couldn't go to camp this year."

"I'm just glad they're back. Maybe I can squeeze a little fun into what's left of summer vacation."

· · · · · · ·

We played double-dutch in the hot sun for about two hours until Tasha remembered that she had to go to her aunt's house. She hadn't said a word to me the whole time, but we did turn rope for each other.

Soon everybody had gone home, and Kelly and I walked back to our block alone. "Tasha and I are going shopping for school supplies tomorrow afternoon. Then we're going roller-skating. Want to come?"

Even though I knew I had major reading to do, I said, "Sure." The last thing I wanted was for Kelly and Tasha to spend more time together without me. I could always read on Monday.

· · · · · · ·

When I woke up on Monday, Mom was on the phone with Dad's mother, who lives in Florida. Mom usually calls her on the holidays because they're the hardest to deal with now that Dad's gone.

"Hold on, Margaret. Delaney's awake now." She handed me the phone.

I covered the mouthpiece with my hand and whispered, "Did you tell her about Dr. Cahill?"

She nodded.

"Why? It's going to make her sad."

"She asked me if I was seeing anybody. Did you want me to lie? Anyway, she said she's glad I'm getting on with my life."

Grandma was probably just saying that so Mom wouldn't feel bad.

I talked to Grandma for a few minutes, telling her all about the job. She said she had seen the commercial we had done already and was looking forward to seeing the show next week. When I got off the phone I asked Mom if she and Dr. Cahill had any plans for the day.

"Well, no. Joshua is spending the day with Bryce and Peg."

I leaned on the counter. "Does it bother you that he still spends time with his ex-wife?"

"Not at all. They share custody of Bryce, so it's good that they can do things as a family every now and then."

Mom was too perfect. I don't think I'd be that understanding if I was in her shoes. "So, what are we going to do today?" I asked.

"Well, every store in the city is having a big Labor Day sale. Want to shop till we drop?"

"Okay. And why don't we invite Neema?"

Mom smiled. "Good idea."

· · · · · · ·

Mom, Neema, and I spent the whole afternoon shopping. The two of them were talking, but there was definitely tension there. It just wasn't the same.

Afterward, we all went back to our apartment, and Mom invited Neema to stay for dinner. She said okay since her husband was still out playing tennis. But Neema isn't a vegetarian, and she wished she had a thick steak to go with the Spanish rice and beans Mom made.

While we were eating, Dr. Cahill stopped by on his way home and Mom asked him to stay for dinner.

"I never turn down a free meal," he joked, taking a seat next to Neema.

"Do you think this is a good idea?" I whispered to Mom while she prepared his plate. "I mean Neema and Dr. Cahill in the same room?"

"Why don't we wait and see what happens, Delaney? Maybe Neema will feel differently once she gets to know him." She set the plate in front of him.

"This would be perfect with a nice juicy steak," he said.

"That's what I was telling her," Neema said.

Mom put her hands on her hips. "One more word out of either of you and I'll take my food back and send you both home hungry."

They both laughed. Everyone got along great after that, even Neema and Dr. Cahill. During the meal I glanced at Mom, and she gave me a wink. Things were going better than planned.

When Dr. Cahill left, Neema said to Mom, "I guess I can see why you like Joshua. He's a very nice man."

Mom began clearing the dishes. "But you still don't think we should date, right?"

"I'm sorry. That's just the way I feel. And you're going to run into a lot of people who feel the same way."

"We know," Mom said. "And we're prepared."

Both of them looked at me. I guess I shouldn't have been eavesdropping. I understood how both of them felt. I just didn't know which one I agreed with.

"Sorry," I mumbled.

Mom shook her head. "Delaney is always listening to my conversations. I really have to watch what I say around her."

I hate when she talks about me as if I'm not there.

While Neema waited for her husband to pick her up, she and Mom laughed like old friends again. Why was it so easy for them to make up and so difficult for Tasha and me?

· · · · · · ·

That evening I still had a lot of reading to do. And I had to memorize the questions to ask and in what order. I went into my room and sat on the floor, trying to force the information into my brain, but I was so tired I couldn't concentrate. It was my fault; I had done this to myself.

At nine o'clock I started to get nervous and my head began to hurt. I'd read the folder, but I couldn't remember most of the stuff. I thought of all the time I had spent with Kelly over the weekend, playing, shopping, and skating when I should have been doing work. But then I might have lost Kelly's friendship.

It was tough trying to choose between my job and my best friend. All I knew was that Kathleen, Cory, and I would be doing our first interview with a big star tomorrow, and I wasn't as prepared as I should be.

IO

. . . .

Billy Denim was staying at the New York Hilton, which is only about ten blocks from the network building. Since we were so excited about meeting him, we decided to walk. We needed time to calm down.

It was almost one o'clock, and the afternoon was overcast and gray. I hoped it wouldn't rain before we got to the hotel because I was all dressed up in a beige dress with brown accessories and sandals. The hair stylist had brushed my hair into a very sophisticated style, one that needed a lot of mousse. I was already in makeup, so I looked much older.

On the way to the hotel, we talked and giggled nonstop. Cory kept talking about what a terrific musician Billy Denim was, but all Lauren, Kathleen, and I said was how great he looked and how cool he was.

The hotel was very fancy, with crystal chandeliers and marble floors. There were about twenty teenage girls hanging around the lobby, obviously fans waiting to catch a glimpse of Billy Denim. We took the elevator up to the twelfth floor, where Mike was waiting for us outside Billy's suite. My hands were sweaty. Cory whispered to me, "Do you think he'll play a song for us?"

"That would be great."

We walked into the suite. There was a kitchen, a living room, and a door leading to another room. Cameras and lights were set up in front of the sofa, and there were a lot of people in the room. But there was no Billy Denim.

Lauren pulled us into a huddle. "Remember, troops, we are here to do a job, and we are going to behave entirely like professionals. This shouldn't take more than an hour or so."

"Where's Billy?" Kathleen asked.

"He's in his bedroom. The man in the gray suit is Billy's manager, Gus."

Gus, who was standing in the doorway to Billy's room, looked frustrated. A few minutes later he held up his hands and announced, "Billy wants me to tell you folks that he'll be ready for the interview right after 'All My Children.' "

Everyone's mouth flew open at the same time. "You mean he expects us to wait while he catches up on his soap operas?" I asked. My voice was way too loud, and Lauren and Mike gave me shocked looks.

Lauren put her finger to her lips. "Ssh, Delaney. Are you trying to blow this whole interview?"

I took a seat on the sofa and watched as Mike made sure all the cameras and lights were properly arranged. At two o'clock Gus knocked on the door. This time I could hear Billy say, "I'm coming, man."

Fifteen minutes later Gus knocked on the door again,

and this time Billy yelled, "I'm getting dressed, man. Don't get your blood pressure up."

Gus told us all to be patient again. "Billy had a long night last night. He played to a sold-out crowd at Madison Square Garden."

Cory sat down next to me. "Are we having fun yet?"

"Can't you tell?"

Kathleen said, "I'm sure it'll be worth the wait. We'll be able to tell all our friends we actually talked to Billy Denim."

I didn't say anything to that. I just hoped I could get through this interview without messing up.

When Billy finally came out of the bedroom a half hour later, he wasn't wearing a shirt, he hadn't shaved, and he was smoking a cigarette. Kathleen sighed like a lovesick dog. Cory and I just stared. Gus said to him, "Billy, you're doing an interview. You need a shirt."

Lauren leaned over and whispered, "Great body!"

"You said it," Kathleen said.

Billy and Gus argued about the shirt for five minutes. Then the two of them went into the bedroom for about fifteen minutes. When Billy came out, he was the Billy Denim I knew. He had on jeans, a black T-shirt, and a white bandanna around his head. His long dark hair was still messy, and he still hadn't shaved, but he looked incredibly handsome.

Kathleen sighed again. "It should be against the law for any man to be that gorgeous!"

Lauren and Mike went over and shook his hand. They talked for a few minutes, but it didn't seem as if Billy really wanted to be bothered with any of this. Then Lauren turned around and waved for us to join her. We stood up and walked over slowly.

"Billy, I'd like you to meet Delaney Crawford and Cory Drennen."

First he shook Cory's hand. Then he held his hand out for mine. As he clasped it, I silently prayed my hand wouldn't feel sweaty to him. He shook quickly and said, "Yeah."

"And this is Kathleen Sutherland," Lauren said.

Only Billy didn't offer his hand to her. Instead he put his arm around her waist and said, "How are you doing, pretty darling?"

Kathleen giggled. "I'm doing great, handsome."

I couldn't believe it. He was actually flirting with her.

Lauren gently pulled Kathleen away, saying, "Kathleen is fourteen years old."

Billy got the hint. He held up his hands and said, "Relax. That's cool."

A few minutes later we were all seated in front of the bright lights. Kathleen and I were sitting on either side of Billy, and Cory was sitting on the arm of the sofa next to me.

Billy was puffing on another cigarette, and the smoke was going up in my nose and mouth. He didn't stop smoking until the second before the videotape started running. Mike yelled, "Okay, people. Action!"

Kathleen started the questioning as we had rehearsed. "Billy Denim, you're one of the most famous lead singers in the country right now. When you were a young boy did you dream of becoming a singer?"

Billy shook his head and said, "No." And that was it.

"What did you want to be?"

"I don't know," he said. Then he stood up and said, "I have to go to the bathroom. I'll be back, man."

I was getting frustrated. It was almost four o'clock and Billy had no idea that we had better things to do than wait for him. When he came back, it was my turn to ask him a question. "What made you write the song 'Don't Even Start'?"

"I wanted kids to know that they don't have to start doing drugs to be cool. I never did, and look at me."

"That's a great message," Kathleen said. "And it's a great song. I hope everyone takes your advice."

At that moment the door to the suite opened and a man called out, "What's going on, Billy? You dudes having a party and didn't invite me?" His blond hair was oily and long, and he was wearing jeans and a torn army jacket.

Again Billy got up. He went over and talked to his friend while Cory whispered, "That's Shake Emerson, the drummer."

"He looks like a bum," I said.

"Don't you know anything about fashion?" Kathleen asked.

Billy and Shake talked and laughed for about ten minutes until Gus went over to them and reminded Billy that he was in the middle of an interview. Before Billy sat down again, he lit up another cigarette and smoked all of it.

Then Cory asked, "How does it feel to have the number-one song on the Billboard chart?"

"It feels cool, man! Wait until I release my next song, 'Prime-time Girl.' You'll love it, man!"

As we struggled on with the interview, Billy received two phone calls which he insisted on taking, had another visitor, and smoked four more cigarettes. While Billy was talking to Shake in the hallway, Lauren called room service for a platter of snacks. It was after six o'clock, and none of us had eaten for hours.

We waited until six-thirty and the food still hadn't come. Lauren called downstairs again. I heard her say, "Well, we never got it. They must have delivered it to the wrong room."

At that moment Billy returned from the hallway and said, "Whoever ordered the food, it was pretty cool. Except for the cheese dip. That processed stuff is no good for you. They put a lot of chemicals in it."

Lauren shook her head and apologized to the man on the phone.

The rest of the interview went by with only two more cigarette breaks. Finally Mike said, "Okay, kids. That's good enough."

Billy jumped up and walked straight into his bedroom without even saying good-bye to us. Gus followed him.

I couldn't hold my tongue any longer. "Billy Denim is a jerk!"

"Yeah, but he's cute," Kathleen said. As usual, she had a one-track mind.

"That's true," I admitted. "But he's still a jerk!"

· · · · · · ·

"Bryce was in the office today," Mom said. It was after dinner, and we were lying in her bed together. Mom was watching some gross medical show on PBS, and I was reading my info pack on Wendy Newman. We were also pigging out on carrot cake. "I asked him if he would be interested in a part-time job, and he said yes."

"Doing what?"

"Picking you up after school and taking you to rehearsal."

I almost choked. "I hardly know him. How could you do that without even asking me?"

Mom gave me one of her looks. "Since when do I need your permission? I thought I was the mother and you were the child."

"Oh, I get it. You're just hiring him because he's Dr. Cahill's son."

"That has nothing to do with it, Miss know-it-all. He really wants to earn some money, so he jumped at the chance to take you to work." The program Mom was watching ended, and she reached for the remote control and turned it off.

"Dr. Cahill gives Bryce an allowance, right?" I asked. "So why does he need so much extra money?"

"He told me he's saving up for something big, but he wouldn't tell me what it was."

When we'd finished the cake, Mom took the dishes into the kitchen. I followed her to get some water. "It's time for bed, don't you think?" she asked, loading the dishwasher.

"It's only ten o'clock, and I'm off tomorrow."

"But you have a lot of reading to do."

"It won't take that long. I can finish reading it in the morning and then spend the afternoon with Kelly."

"That's what you said before, and you waited until the last minute. No. Tomorrow you're coming to the office with me, and you're going to spend the day reading and preparing."

"Mom—"

"Don't 'Mom' me. Before I allowed you to accept this job, you told me that you knew there would be sacrifices, but you thought it was worth it."

I hate when she brings back my words to haunt me.

"You're the one who wanted to take this job. Did I pressure you into it? Did I drag you to auditions all summer against your will?"

"No."

"The network is paying you very well, and they deserve to have you give one hundred percent to everything you do." She kissed me good night. "I'll wake you up at seven-thirty."

As I lay in bed that night I thought about Kelly and Tasha, who would probably spend the entire day together while I sat in Mom's office reading. The two of them were getting closer and closer, and I was getting farther away. I was beginning to agree with Kathleen, of all people. This was the worst summer of my life.

▌▌

On Thursday Mom knocked on my door at exactly three-thirty in the morning. "It's that time, Delaney."

I turned over and curled up in a little ball. "Fifteen more minutes," I begged. It just wasn't normal to get up at that hour.

Mom opened the door. "You have to be at the studio in an hour and a half. I suggest you get up now."

I grunted.

That's when she turned on the light.

"Aarghh!"

"Come on, Delaney. Do you want to be called into Ms. Seachman's office?"

Mom had done it again. I was awake instantly. Then I started to get excited. Today was the day I taped my very own segment.

It was still dark outside when we arrived at the studio. Mom came upstairs with me for the first time. She's usually afraid that people will think she's a stage mother.

We ran into Lauren in the hallway. "Breakfast is waiting in your dressing room," she said. "I'll be in to give you last-minute instructions before you go."

"Aren't you coming with me?"

"No, I'm working with Kathleen on her fashion show today. We got permission to videotape it at the Statue of Liberty." She saw my expression, which may have looked a little jealous. "I'll go with you next week."

I smiled.

Mom and I went into my dressing room. A platter was set up on my makeup table with enough food for a family of four. "Does Fran really expect me to eat all of this?" I asked.

"Eat the bran muffin at least," Mom said. "And have some milk."

"But I already had a glass at home. Can't a person have too much protein?"

"Not a vegetarian. Drink."

After breakfast we went down the hallway, and Mom met Penny and the makeup artists. It was nice having her there to help me get ready and fuss over me the way she did when I was little.

"How do I look?" I asked Mom, spinning around. I was wearing an off-white skirt with a red shirt and red flat shoes.

"Cute," Mom said.

"Cute?"

"Cute," she repeated.

That's when Lauren walked into the dressing room. "Delaney, you look so cute." She handed me a pile of folded clothes. "Pack these things in your knapsack. Mike is waiting for you by the elevator."

As I shoved the sweat suit and leotards into my bag, Mom wished me good luck. Then we were on our way.

· · · · · · ·

Wendy Newman lived in Queens, about a half hour away from the studio in Mahattan. Outside the van window I watched the city disappear and trees and grass appear. Sometimes I wish I lived in a suburban area, in a beautiful house with a big backyard. Everything looked so peaceful.

"This is it," Mike said, opening the van's two back doors. He helped me onto the street and I waited while the crew unloaded the cameras and lighting equipment. Then, when everybody was ready, Mike told me to go up and ring the doorbell.

"By myself?"

"We'll be right behind you. Whatever you do, don't look into the cameras. Pretend we're not here."

The two cameramen were carrying heavy equipment with wires everywhere. It would be difficult pretending they weren't there. "What if I mess up or get tongue-tied?"

"If you mess up real bad, we'll cut that part out of the tape. Come on, Delaney, have fun with this."

I hurried up the walk and rang the bell. Wendy's grandmother answered the door. According to the info pack, Wendy had come to live with her grandmother over the summer so she could train with a new coach. She had left her parents and five brothers and sisters back in Indiana.

"Wendy's upstairs in her room," she said. "You can go up."

"Thank you."

I turned to Mike, forgetting that I wasn't supposed to

look into the camera. He said, "Go upstairs and introduce yourself. Then when she's ready we'll tape her leaving for the arena."

Wendy was sitting on her bedroom floor sorting through a bunch of cassette tapes. She didn't look innocent like in her picture in the info pack. Here her long brown hair was wavy and wild looking. And she was wearing jeans that were covered with patches of different rock groups.

She looked up. "Oh, I didn't know you guys were here already."

"They're downstairs waiting for you," I said, then added, "Oh, I'm Delaney Crawford."

"I know. Your executive producer told me all about you."

I joined her on the floor. "What are you doing?"

"Trying to find some music to work out to. If I don't bring anything my trainer plays something that sounds twenty years old."

"Do you have the new Billy Denim tape?"

"Yeah. That's a good idea." She dug for it in the pile. "We'll be able to work up a real sweat to this."

"We'll?"

She laughed. "You'll love high-impact aerobics! Just wait." She jumped up. "I'll be ready in a second."

I looked through her tape collecton while she packed her duffel bag. She liked a lot of the same groups that I did.

"You can borrow anything you like," she said. "That way we'll get to see each other again."

"Okay, thanks."

I found two tapes I didn't have and stood up. "Do you want me to put the rest of them away?"

"Nah, leave them there. I'll just mess them up again tomorrow."

She stood at her mirror and began brushing her hair. "Do you think I need more makeup?"

"No, you're okay. Did you put it on yourself?"

"Yeah. I know how because I wear it during competition. If you want I could show you how to put on mascara and blush."

"My mother would kill me," I said. "She says I can't wear makeup off camera until high school."

"That's weird. I thought New York girls got to wear makeup in kindergarten."

"Someone forgot to tell my mother that."

Before we left the room, Wendy grabbed my hand. "I'm scared," she said. "I thought this feeling in my stomach would go away, but it's not."

"There's nothing to be worried about," I told her, hoping I sounded convincing. "Just be yourself."

"Be myself," she repeated, and took a few quick breaths. "Okay, I think I'm ready now. Please let this day go by quickly!"

· · · · · · ·

Needless to say, the day didn't go very quickly at all, but Wendy and I got along so great we didn't care. She was the coolest person I had ever met.

"Paris is the best city on earth," she said in the locker room. We had just finished working out with her trainer, Gabriel, and now we had to change our clothes. "I was there last year for the Junior World Competition. The people are so cultured and sophisticated. You wouldn't believe it."

"I wish I could travel to a different country," I said. "My problem is that my parents took me everywhere when I was too young to remember."

"Bummer."

I stuffed my sweat suit into my knapsack and put on my black tights and red leotard. Compared to Wendy's outfit, mine looked pretty plain. Hers had colorful zigzags and swirls all over it and looked really neat.

We sat on the bench and laced up our skates. "Isn't it kind of weird to ice-skate in the summer?" I asked.

"Not for me. I've been ice-skating year-round since I was four."

I shook my head and laughed.

"Come on," she said, standing up. "It's time to face the ice."

When we got to the rink, Mike called me over to where he was standing. "So far so good," he said. "Warm up with her on the ice until she's ready to work with her coach. Then we'll get out of the way for a while. We don't want to interfere with her training."

"If I fall will you cut that out of the tape?"

"No way!"

Wendy and I went onto the ice. I lasted on my feet for about ten seconds, then *splatt*! When I looked up, I saw one of the cameramen pointing the camera right at me. That would definitely be part of the segment.

"How could you fall so quickly?" Wendy asked, helping me up.

I flopped around for a few minutes until I regained my balance. It had been a long time since I had been ice-skating.

We warmed up for ten minutes, skating around and

around until I felt dizzy. Then Wendy's coach, Sandy, came onto the ice. "We have a lot of work today," she told Wendy. "The opening part of your routine still looks sloppy."

"Have fun," I said, and skated away. Right before I reached the side of the rink, I fell again. And again when I looked up, a camera was pointed in my direction. This was going to be some segment with me falling all over the place. We might as well call it A Day in the Life of a Klutz!

I had an hour break while the crew videotaped Wendy. She and her coach ran through her routine about ten times, until Wendy looked as if she was about to drop. But after each time, Sandy would say, "Watch your lines," or "Extend yourself."

I had no idea what she was talking about. From where I stood, the routine looked perfect. Wendy was a very graceful skater.

A little while later Wendy attempted a double axle. She jumped in the air, spun around twice, but fell when she landed. Sandy wasn't sympathetic. She said, "Do you see what you're doing wrong? Okay, take a break."

Wendy got up and limped to the side where we were standing.

"Are you okay?" I asked.

"I'm fine. Just having a hard time keeping my body straight in the air." She sat on a bench and I joined her.

Mike came over and handed me a microphone. "Do a little interviewing, Delaney," he said.

Both cameramen came over and began taping us.

"Whenever you're ready," Mike said.

"Is skating fun?" I asked Wendy. "I mean, you have to keep doing the same thing over and over."

I pointed the microphone in her direction. "It's hard work," she said. "But I guess it's fun. I like competing, so I have to put a lot of time into practicing."

"I read that you had to move away from your home to train here in New York. That must have been difficult."

"It was. My whole family lives in Indiana, and I really loved it there. But I needed a coach who could take me on to the Olympics." She shook her hair out of her face. "Delaney, I want an Olympic gold medal so bad I can taste it."

"Okay, girls," Mike said. "That's good enough for now. Relax."

"You were good, Wendy," I said when the cameras stopped rolling. "I think you're getting the hang of this."

"I'm too tired to be nervous." She laughed. "Let me get back on the ice before Sandy gets upset. I'll be done in about forty minutes."

· · · · · · ·

We had lunch at a little diner near the arena. Mike had already gotten permission to videotape there, so they were expecting us. Wendy and I sat at a table together, and we both ordered salads and milk shakes.

"I can't eat with a camera on me," Wendy whispered. "Suppose I dribble?"

I started laughing.

She picked up a crouton and threw it at me. "Don't laugh! I'm serious. I can just see it now. 'Junior champion skater dribbles salad dressing. Film at eleven'!"

I picked up the crouton and threw it back at her. "You are so silly!"

After lunch we had to go into Manhattan to Wendy's dance class. There were only three other girls in her class, two gymnasts and another figure skater. I put my leotard back on and joined the ballet class for a few minutes, but I didn't understand any of the French words the instructor was saying so I dropped out before totally embarrassing myself.

So while the cameramen taped the class, I leaned against the barre and watched. The instructor was very strict. She kept saying, "You have to work harder if you want to be the best. Harder, harder, harder."

After the class Mike told me to do some more interviewing, so I asked Wendy why she had to take ballet lessons.

"It strengthens my body and teaches me how to be graceful."

"How does it make you feel when your instructor keeps telling you to work harder?"

"We need her to push us. There are good skaters all over the world. Only one can be the best."

I would have headaches every day if I had that kind of pressure on me.

By the end of the day I was exhausted. After ballet class Wendy had to go for a costume fitting, then we went back to the ice arena where Wendy worked with both Sandy and her choreographer for another couple of hours. Then around seven o'clock we all went back to her house to do some more videotaping. She showed us some of the trophies and medals she had won.

"I couldn't bring them all with me," she said. "These are my favorites."

"Can you stay for dinner, Delaney?" Wendy's grandmother asked me.

I looked at Mike. "Go ahead," he said.

While Wendy, her grandmother, and I ate, the camera never stopped rolling. "You pack a lot of stuff into a day," I said to Wendy across the table. "How many days a week do you do all of this?"

"Five. On Saturdays I'm on the ice all day."

"I guess you have to be dedicated."

She nodded. "There's no other way."

Before we left Wendy and I exchanged phone numbers and promised to keep in touch. "I mean it," she said. "I haven't made any friends since I moved here. You're the first one."

"I'll call you after the show airs," I said. "To see if you liked your segment."

• • • • • • •

I had to go back to the network building and change, then Lauren and Eric dropped me home. Mom was at the kitchen counter making out the paychecks for her employees when I got there. "I was starting to get worried," she said.

"It's only nine-thirty and I'm off tomorrow." I poured myself a glass of milk before I was told to and sat down across from Mom. "Can I help you?"

"No, I'm just about done. Besides, I want to hear how your day went."

I told her every detail of what had happened and how

nice Wendy was. "I don't know how she can keep that kind of schedule. I'd be wiped out."

Mom packed up her work. "Speaking of schedules, I have to discuss something very important with you."

I followed her into her room. On her bed was a manila envelope. She handed it to me. "I want you to look this over. It's information on the Saxon School for Professional Children."

I opened up the envelope and flipped through the school brochure. "What does this have to do with me?"

"Before I left the network this morning, Ms. Seachman and I went over your schedule for the next couple of weeks. She's afraid it'll be too hard if you stay at your school. If you transfer to the Saxon School, you'll only have to go four hours a day, and you'll receive tutoring on the set."

My mouth flew open. "No! You can't make me leave my school!"

"*I'm* not making you do anything, Delaney. I'm not all that crazy about this situation. I want you to have the same quality of education that you've always had."

"Good, then forget about this school." I tossed the brochure on her bed.

"But I don't want you to be exhausted everyday either. I want what's best for you." .

"Staying in school with my friends is what's best for me," I told her. "Trust me, it's going to be okay."

12

··

Mom had a date the following evening, so I went to Kelly's house to help her baby-sit Lynn. Her mother had gone to the airport to pick up her father, and they weren't due back until around eight.

"I wish you were going to be around this weekend," Kelly said. "Dad's taking me to the movies tomorrow afternoon. And on Sunday we're going to a doubleheader baseball game. He said I could invite whoever I wanted."

"Who's going?" I asked. "As if I don't know."

"I asked Tasha already, but she has a hair appointment tomorrow and she's busy Sunday."

"You asked her before me?"

"You're never around anymore. And I knew you were going to be upstate on your fossil dig this weekend."

I sighed. "This is our last day together before school starts. Let's do something."

"I'm stuck with Lynn, remember?"

I was totally bored. "She's sleeping. We have to do something."

"We can cook dinner for my parents."

"Yeah! A romantic dinner with candles and soft music." Mr. and Mrs. O'Shea hadn't seen each other in almost two weeks. It was perfect.

Kelly got out the cookbooks, and we chose a meal quickly. Luckily we didn't need to go out and buy anything. Since we couldn't use the oven without an adult around, we just mixed the ingredients for the eggplant parmesan and then set the table. It looked very romantic.

"Now all we need is the music," I said.

"The discs are in their room." She ran down the hallway, but when she came back she didn't have a disc. She had a book. "Look what I found. I can't believe it!"

The book was called *Growing and Changing*, and it was about how girls develop, get their periods, and become women. And it was loaded with drawings.

"This is going to be good!" I said. We sat down at the kitchen table and flipped through the pages, giggling like crazy. Some of the pictures were really weird looking.

"This is neat," Kelly said. "I never knew we looked like this on the inside."

"Me neither."

She leaned closer to me. "I'm wearing my bra on the first day of school."

"You are?"

"Yeah. I haven't worn it yet. Besides, we're in sixth grade now." She closed the book. "Let's go check on the baby. We can read this later."

When Kelly's parents came home, Mrs. O'Shea smiled when she saw the book on the table. "I was waiting for the right time to show that to you," she told Kelly. "But since you found it, we'll have to have a long talk about it over the weekend."

"Really?" Kelly looked excited.

We finished cooking, then served dinner to her parents and made sure they had their privacy. Then Mom called at nine-thirty to tell me it was time to come home. I hurried down the block hoping Mom and I could have a girl talk ourselves.

But when I got into my apartment, she wasn't alone. Dr. Cahill was there.

"How was your evening?" Mom asked me. The two of them were sitting at the kitchen counter having tea.

"It was okay. Hello, Dr. Cahill." I forced a smile.

Mom kissed me. "You have to get up early tomorrow. Why don't you hit the bed now?"

"Um, I have to make sure I packed everything."

"Okay, but don't stay up late."

I went down the hallway to my room feeling as if she was trying to get rid of me. A few minutes later I went out to the kitchen again. "Mom, did you buy me one of those little tubes of toothpaste?"

"Oh, I forgot. Just take one of the regular ones from the hall closet."

I left, packed the toothpaste in my knapsack, then returned to the kitchen. "I want some water," I said, going to the refrigerator. Slowly, I poured myself a glass and sipped it down.

Mom and Dr. Cahill were talking and laughing like teenagers. They had gone to a jazz concert and were still all dressed up.

After two glasses, Mom said, "Delaney, that's enough

water. I want you to go to bed now so you won't have a hard time getting up in the morning."

"I'm real thirsty," I said, filling up another glass.

Mom stood up, took the glass out of my hand, and poured the water down the sink. "Bed!"

I stamped my feet as I left the room. "I see you've made your choice. Dr. Cahill is the winner!"

I flopped on my bed with my arms folded across my chest. Mom came into my room and shut the door. "Okay, what's the matter?"

"Nothing."

"Do you have a problem?"

"No."

"Good."

She started to leave, so I said, "Is he staying all night?"

Mom stared at me for a long time. "No, he's not. I cut our evening short because I didn't have a sitter for you. It's not even ten o'clock and I'm not ready for this date to end. Can you understand that?"

"Yes," I said angrily.

"Good night. And I don't want you to come back out there."

I didn't move from my spot until I heard Dr. Cahill leave about twenty minutes later. Then I undressed, put on my pajamas, and went down the hall. Mom was in the bathroom washing off her makeup. I stood in the doorway without saying anything.

She patted her face dry with a towel. "Your behavior is going from bad to worse, young lady. I want you to start thinking about what you say before you open your mouth. You really embarrassed me this evening."

She walked past me into her room. I sat on her bed

while she got undressed. "Kelly's mother bought her a book about how girls change and grow," I explained. "I wanted to talk to you about that stuff, but *he* was here. I didn't mean to ruin your date."

"That's funny, because that's exactly what you did."

"But you can spend the whole weekend with him. This is my last day."

She sat next to me. "There is no excuse for how you acted in front of Joshua. I don't understand why you feel you have to compete with him. You're my daughter and I love you. You are the best thing in my life." She kissed me on the forehead. "Now talk to me."

I smiled. "Mom, it's time I got a bra. I mean, I know I don't really need one, but Kelly's wearing hers on Monday. I'll be the last person on earth without one."

"I doubt that."

"Pleeease."

She laughed. "Okay, okay. We'll go shopping next weekend."

I got under her covers. "Mom, I know I have to get up early, but can we at least have part one of girl talk tonight?"

Mom got in bed next to me. "Okay, but I don't want you begging for more time in the morning."

"I promise. I promise."

·······

"Ten more minutes, Mom. Come on." I grabbed the covers and pulled them over my head to hide from her.

"Delaney, you promised."

I sat up with my eyes still shut. "Why do you always remember everything I promise?"

"Because I'm your mother. That's my job." She grabbed the covers off me. "Now let's get a move on."

· · · · · · ·

The studio was bubbling with activity when we got there at six o'clock. There were a lot of people rushing around making last minute preparations for our trip to Letchworth State Park. And to make matters worse, Kathleen was late.

While Mom talked with Cory's parents in the hallway, Cory asked me, "Do you think we're finally going to meet Diana Sutherland?"

"I hope so. But she might be busy filming somewhere."

"My dad rented one of her old movies. She was real pretty, just like Kathleen. I wonder what she looks like now."

But when Kathleen arrived, her mother wasn't with her. Her older sister, Jeanette, was. Ms. Seachman took Kathleen aside and chewed her out for a few minutes, the same treatment she had given me. When Kathleen tried to explain why she was late, Ms. Seachman didn't want to hear it.

"All right, troops," Lauren said. "We have a plane to catch."

Mom and I hugged. "Call me when you get there," she said.

I looked up at her and there were tears in her eyes. "Don't worry," I said. "I'll be okay." It's hard for us to say good-bye, even if it's just for a weekend. It makes us think about Dad, who just said good-bye one day and we never got to see him again.

Since Mike and the camera crew had left the night before, only five of us were going: we three kids, Lauren, and Eric, who was going to chaperone Cory. On the way to the airport Cory started getting nervous because he had never been on a plane before. He named every plane disaster film he had ever seen and wouldn't listen when we told him that those were just movies.

On the plane Kathleen and I sat on either side of Cory and held his hands as we taxied down the runway and took off. After a minute, he leaned forward and looked out the window. "Hey, this is cool!"

Kathleen and I looked at each other and smiled. That was what we had been trying to tell him.

When the pilot told us it was okay to remove the seat belts, Kathleen whispered to us, "Let's spy on Lauren and Eric." They were seated behind us and we hadn't heard a word from them since we boarded.

Quietly we turned around and knelt on our seats. When we looked over the back we caught the two of them making out.

I giggled. "Kissy, kissy, kissy!"

Lauren and Eric jumped apart, looking totally embarrassed.

"Not very professional, Lauren," Kathleen teased. "Aren't you supposed to be doing paperwork or something?"

"Oh, hush." Lauren laughed.

"Way to go, Eric," Cory said and the two of them high fived. "You have to give me lessons, man."

Kathleen and I looked at each other. Then at the same time we started tickling Cory and ruffling his hair. We were laughing so loud the flight attendant had to come over and tell us to quiet down.

When she left, Cory wanted to know what would have happened if we hadn't quieted down.

"They throw you out," Kathleen teased. "Didn't you know that?"

His eyes widened. "Out of the plane?" He leaned forward to look out of the window. Kathleen and I could hardly keep from laughing.

· · · · · · ·

We all called home from the airport in Rochester, then Eric rented a car and drove us to Letchworth State Park. The campsite was already crowded with families cooking out and playing games around the log cabins. We met up with the camera crew, who had already picked out two cabins for us, and the afternoon was spent videotaping us settling in, eating, and exploring in the woods. The park was gorgeous. And there was so much to see.

Later, we hiked up a big rock that overlooked a deep river valley that the local people call the Grand Canyon of the East. It was breathtaking. We stood at the railing, just gazing at it with our mouths open. The clay red sides of the canyon looked purple in the evening sun.

But more than anything, the best thing about the day was how nice Kathleen was. She laughed and joked with us as if it were something she always did. Even when we weren't videotaping.

That night after the taping ended, the three of us sat in front of the girls' cabin and talked under the open sky. Beside a tree several feet away Lauren and Eric held hands and whispered to each other. They made a perfect couple. When it started getting real dark Lauren and Eric told us it was time to turn in. Kathleen and I said good night to Cory and went inside our cabin.

Once we were dressed for bed, the three of us sat on our sleeping bags. "Guess what?" Lauren said, smiling from ear to ear. "Eric asked me to marry him. You two are the first to know."

In the semidarkness we strained to see her ring. "Wow!" Kathleen said. "That's some rock. Eric *must* be rich."

"Would you guys stop saying that? What makes you think he's rich? Just because he has a nice car and can afford a diamond ring?"

"Yes," I said. "What does he do for a living?"

"Real estate," Lauren said.

Kathleen laughed. "See, he *is* rich!"

We stayed up late talking about love and marriage and babies.

13

An unexpected rain prevented us from doing any taping the next morning, so Eric drove us into a nearby town where we had brunch at a small diner. While we ate Lauren spent close to an hour on the pay phone with Ms. Seachman trying to figure out what to do if the rain didn't stop. We still had to go on our fossil dig before catching a seven-thirty flight back to the city.

"I hope it keeps raining," Cory said, shoving a syrupy forkful of waffles into his mouth. "That way we get to stay up here an extra day and miss school tomorrow."

Kathleen laughed. "Wouldn't that be fun?" She was in a great mood for the second day in a row. "But do you think Lauren would go for it? I mean, we'd throw off her schedule."

Eric shook his head. "She wouldn't be too happy about that."

"There's so much left to do," I said. "We still haven't

seen the movie we're supposed to review or had any real rehearsals."

"How do you think the show will turn out?" Kathleen asked me.

"I think it'll be good."

Lauren got off the phone and told me to call home first. Mom picked up after the first ring.

"Mom, it's me."

"Delaney, is everything okay?"

"I'm fine. But it's raining here so we had to hold off on taping."

"Will you be home tonight?"

"I don't know. We're going to wait and see if it clears up. I'll call you again if we have to stay."

"I miss you," Mom said.

"I miss you, too. Is Dr. Cahill there?"

"No."

"Did you go on a date last night?"

"Yes."

"Do you really miss me?"

"Of course." Mom laughed. "What do you want me to say? That my heart aches for you?"

I smiled. "That sounds more like it."

"I hope the weather clears up," Mom said. "I really do."

"Me too."

After we hung up Cory got on the phone, and Kathleen and I went to the ladies' room together.

"How come your mother didn't drop you off yesterday?" I asked. "Cory and I wanted to meet her."

"Uh, she's out of town. You know, filming and stuff."

"Too bad. Sometimes I think we're never going to see her."

"Don't worry," Kathleen said. "You will."

When we got back Cory was finished with the phone and it was Kathleen's turn. The rain didn't seem to be falling as heavily as before. Maybe it would stop in a little while.

· · · · · · · ·

By two o'clock the rain had become only a light drizzle, so Lauren said we would have to try to make do. Our guide for the fossil dig was Mr. Greene, an archaeologist who taught at a university in the area. He was a big guy with long hair and a bushy beard. Just what you'd expect.

While the crew wrapped most of their equipment in plastic, Kathleen, Cory, and I put on rain slickers and hats. We also had to wear all-weather boots that weighed about five pounds each. We rode to Fall Brook in the network van.

"We're going to have to be extra careful in this weather," Mr. Greene told us on camera. "We'll need to climb that rock over there, and it might be slippery."

Slippery wasn't the word! I slid and fell so many times that when we got on the other side, I looked like the swamp monster covered with mud and leaves. Kathleen had held Mr. Greene's hand so she hadn't fallen once, and Cory was naturally athletic.

"I've never seen you look better, Delaney," Cory said while the camera was on us.

I pretended to strangle him. "Very funny."

"Kids, come over here," Mr. Greene called.

We trekked over to the brook and waded in the ankle-deep water.

"There are plenty of small fossils under the water here," he explained, reaching down and pulling out a broken chip of rock.

We all examined it and held it so that the camera could get a close-up of it. The rock had these funny-shaped shells embedded in it, which Mr. Greene called brachiopods. He told us that they were thousands of years old and pointed out some of the differences between brachiopods and clams.

Later on we found something called a trilobite, an oval-shaped fossil that didn't look like anything else I had ever seen. Cory wanted to find dinosaur bones, but Mr. Greene said it would take more than three kids to dig up something like that.

Instead he took us to his office at the university and showed us all the fossils that he and his students had found at Fall Brook and on digs in other parts of the country. The cameramen went around the room videotaping everything while Mr. Greene answered all our questions. The man knew everything.

Before we knew it, Lauren said it was time to wrap up. It was already four-thirty, and we needed to go back to the cabin and get our stuff, then drive all the way to the airport.

"That was fascinating," I said to Kathleen on the way out to the van. "But I can't wait to get home."

"Speak for yourself, Delaney," she said, and walked ahead of us.

"What's the matter with her?" Cory asked.

I shrugged. "I'm beginning to think she's just plain weird."

"You said it, not me."

· · · · · · ·

Cory wanted the window seat on the plane this time, so Kathleen and I had to sit next to each other. As the plane lifted off, Cory seemed to be having the time of his life.

I turned to Kathleen. "Can you believe this is the same boy who was scared to death yesterday?"

She didn't say anything.

"If you don't want to talk why don't you just say so?"

She sighed loudly like I was annoying her.

"I'm sorry," I said sarcastically. "I forgot my place."

"What's that supposed to mean?"

"It means that people like you think you're too good to speak to us regular people. And when you do speak, we should feel honored, right?"

"Be quiet. You don't even know what you're talking about."

"I know I'm sick and tired of you and your stupid moods."

Lauren got out of her seat and came over to us. "I don't know what this is about," she whispered, "but it had better stop right now. There are a lot of people on this plane and I don't want any rumors going around that the cast of 'Friday Afternoon' cannot get along. It would damage the reputation of our show. Either speak nicely to each other or shut up. Am I making myself clear?"

We both nodded and chose to shut up for the rest of the flight.

. . . .

Mom and Dr. Cahill were already at the network building when we got back there. In the hallway I gave Mom a big hug and kiss. I wanted to tell her about the trip and the fossils we'd found, but Lauren wanted to meet with Kathleen, Cory, and me in the rehearsal room for a short conference.

"You all did a wonderful job this weekend," she said when we were seated on the floor in a circle. "You worked very hard and except for the small incident on the plane, you were very professional. It was a great first trip. I'm proud of you three."

We applauded ourselves.

"Now I need to make up the rehearsal schedule for this week." She turned to me. "Delaney, have you thought about the Saxon School?"

"My mother doesn't want me to go there," I said. It wasn't a complete lie. "She wants me to have more than four hours of school a day."

Lauren looked a little frustrated. "I'm not sure we can schedule all of your A Day in the Life of. . . segments on the weekends. I may have to reassign them to Kathleen or Cory."

"But that's *my* job," I said.

"I'm sorry, Delaney, but no regular school will allow you to be absent once a week. I'll try to arrange them on Saturdays, but I can't promise anything."

I sighed and lowered my head. What was I going to do?

Lauren scheduled rehearsals at four o'clock every afternoon. "And on Wednesday and Thursday you'll have to be here in the morning as well."

Kathleen let out a whiny moan.

"I'm sorry, Kathleen, but we have to rehearse when we're all together. And with Delaney's school hours, those are the only free times."

She was piling the guilt sky-high.

Lauren gave us each a copy of our schedule. Seeing it written out, I got scared that maybe everybody was right. I wouldn't have time to breathe between school and work.

"When do we get our scripts?" Kathleen asked.

"We won't be using scripts. I want you to sound natural on the air, not like you're reading."

When Kathleen and Cory left the room, I told Lauren that I was sorry for causing so much trouble.

"Don't worry about it. We're a team and we have to work around problems together. I do wish your mother would reconsider Saxon. It's an excellent school, and with the tutoring you'll learn just as much there as you will anywhere else."

"I don't want to go there either," I admitted. "It's not only my mother; it's me, too. I've never been to a different school before."

"Delaney, sometimes you have to make—"

"I know, sacrifices, right?" I thought about camp and all the fun I had missed out on all summer. Did I have to sacrifice *everything* to be on this show? I mean, if I gave up my school, what was left?

• • • • • • •

Down the hall Mom and Dr. Cahill were standing by the watercooler talking to Kathleen. "Don't worry," Mom said to her as I approached. "I'm sure she'll be okay."

Kathleen nodded.

"Do you need a lift home, sweetheart?" Dr. Cahill asked her.

"Yes, thank you."

All the way out to the car I wanted to ask Mom what was going on, but I decided to wait until after Kathleen had been dropped off. Parked outside her ritzy Park Avenue apartment building, Mom and I waited while Dr. Cahill escorted her upstairs.

"What's wrong with Kathleen?" I asked Mom.

"You don't know?"

I leaned forward. "No."

"Her mother checked herself into an alcohol treatment center yesterday. It was all over the news."

"Diana Sutherland is an alcoholic?" My mouth hung open.

"Apparently. When they showed her on television she didn't look anything like the woman who starred in those movies several years ago." Mom shook her head. "I guess once her career started slipping, there was nothing else for her to do."

"No wonder Kathleen comes to work with such a bad attitude all the time," I said, sitting back in my seat. Kathleen had been so friendly during Saturday's taping, almost as if she was glad to be away from home. But after she had called home, she changed. Now it all made sense. Why did I have to pick a fight with her?

"All I know is this whole thing has made me quite worried about you, Delaney," Mom said.

"Me?"

"Yes. I don't want you to build your whole future on

show business. I want you to have a good education so that if things don't work out, you'll always be able to do something else."

"So it's okay if I don't want to go to the Saxon School?"

"It's fine with me. Just as long as you promise to tell me if things get too hard for you."

"I promise," I said, and kissed Mom excitedly. "Thanks."

14

. . . .

"Hurry up, Delaney!" Mom called from the kitchen. "You're going to be late."

I was in my room on my knees trying to see if my left shoe was under the bed. "One minute," I shouted, hoping she wouldn't come into my room and find me wearing only one shoe. I knew exactly what she would say. "Didn't I tell you to lay out your clothes and shoes when we got home last night? Why don't you ever listen to me? If you had done what I said, you wouldn't be in this predicament now, would you?"

I know Mom like the back of my hand.

The shoe was behind my desk, underneath an overdue library book that I had completely forgotten about.

"Delaney! The girls are going to be waiting for you."

"I'm coming, I'm coming." I slipped on the shoe and took a final glance at myself in my full-length mirror. In my blue-and-white school uniform I looked okay. Not special, just okay. I grabbed my knapsack and hurried out of my room.

Outside, the morning was sunny and warm. I went to Kelly's house first and picked her up, then the two of us headed over to Tasha's. The last thing I wanted to do was walk to school with Tasha, but it was sort of a tradition.

"Lynn cried all night," Kelly said as we crossed the street.

"When did she start doing that again?"

"She never stopped." She giggled. "Oh yeah. I'm wearing my bra. Can you tell?"

I couldn't, but I told her I could. Then we rang Tasha's doorbell. Her father answered it. "She's not ready yet," he told us. "She spilled cranberry juice on her uniform blouse. She's changing."

We went into Tasha's room and sat on her bed. Tasha was standing there in just her underwear and socks, going through her closet. Kelly and I looked at each other, amazed. Tasha was really built. She had already outgrown her training bra and was wearing a *real* one.

"Am I the only one who's nervous about starting sixth grade?" Kelly asked.

"There's nothing to be nervous about," Tasha said. "We've been in school with the same kids since kindergarten." She put on another uniform blouse and then stepped into her uniform dress and buttoned it at the shoulder and waist. "Let's go."

We walked up Fifth Avenue quickly to make up the time we had lost. Our school was on Twenty-third Street near Broadway, but since city blocks are pretty short, it's not a very far walk. It only takes about fifteen minutes.

"Let's all sit together," Kelly said when we got to our classroom. Since the teacher hadn't arrived yet, the place was going crazy.

"The teacher will separate us if we talk," I said. "We'll have to be careful.'"

"Let's sit in the back and pass notes," Kelly said, pointing out three seats near the window.

"No," Tasha said. "If we sit in the back, the teacher will think we're going to cause trouble. Then she'll watch us all the time. The best place to sit is somewhere in the middle."

We found seats. I sat behind Tasha and across from Kelly.

At the door, Gina Foster was shamelessly flirting with a tall seventh grader. She was laughing and twirling her hair around her finger.

"I see Gina's starting early this year," I said.

Tasha turned around in her seat, "What does that mean? Is there something wrong with liking a boy?"

"Are you talking to me?" I asked.

"Gosh, you are so immature, Delaney. Sometimes it's hard to believe we're the same age."

The teacher walked into the classroom. Kelly leaned over. "Would you two cut it out? We don't want to be separated on the first day."

Everyone in the room took a seat quickly and quietly. This teacher didn't look particularly friendly. She looked stern, like a military woman.

I guess I expected the first day to be easy, like write an essay on how we spent summer vacation and stuff like that, but not with Mrs. Hoffman. After she handed out the textbooks, she told us we'd be covering all subjects today and we would have homework. Everyone groaned. No teacher gave homework on the first day of school.

At lunchtime Tasha and Kelly made plans to do their homework together after school. I had rehearsal, so I felt totally left out. I looked away to the next table where the boys in my class were mixing their food and milk together and stirring it around. They were doing the same thing they had done in fourth and fifth grades. Boys never grow up.

· · · · · · ·

Bryce was waiting outside the school for me at three o'clock. I waved good-bye to Kelly and watched as she went down the street with Tasha.

"Do we have time to walk?" Bryce asked. "I want to stop off at this pet store on Thirty-fourth Street."

"Walk? From here to Times Square? That's twenty blocks!"

"Come on. I'll carry your knapsack." I handed it to him, and he slipped it over one arm. "Of course now I look ridiculous carrying a girl's bag."

"You volunteered." I laughed.

The pet store was called The Lily Pad, and it specialized in reptiles and amphibians. "That's the one I want," Bryce said pointing to a big, ugly iguana in a gigantic tank. "His name is Grendel, and he's over two feet long."

"Gross!" I said, though I couldn't take my eyes off the thing. There were bumps all over his green back and tail, and he had orange webbed feet.

With his face just a few inches from the glass, Bryce stared at the iguana as though he were hypnotized. "I've been saving up for him for a month," he said. "With this job, I'll be able to get him real soon."

The turtle-shaped clock on the wall read three-forty. "Bryce, I'm going to be late."

He didn't budge.

"Come on!" I grabbed hold of his wrist and dragged him out of the store.

· · · · · · ·

I didn't have a chance to talk to Kathleen at first because while she worked with one of the associate producers on her Listen Up! segment, I had to do the voice-over for the Wendy Newman piece.

Lauren and I took the elevator up to the fifty-sixth floor. We walked down a dark hallway with rooms on either side of us. Above some of the doors were red lit signs that read QUIET—ON THE AIR.

"Where are we?" I whispered to Lauren. "The twilight zone?"

She laughed. "No, nothing that interesting. The network owns a radio station that broadcasts from this building. We'll be using one of their recording booths this afternoon for your voice-over."

Inside the recording studio were three glass booths, two of them occupied. Waiting for us was a woman who Lauren introduced to me as Sally, the sound engineer on the show. When I asked her what that meant, she said she ran the soundboard and pointed to a huge, black, electronic thing that had about a hundred different levers and switches on it.

"You really know how to work this thing?" I asked.

She nodded.

"Wow. My mother doesn't even know how to program the VCR!"

Both she and Lauren laughed.

A few minutes later Lauren handed me some sheets of paper, and I went inside the empty booth and took a seat on the stool. Lauren and Sally were facing me on the other side of the glass. I looked around. The only other thing in there was a microphone hanging from the ceiling in front of me.

"Read the script naturally," Lauren told me. "If you mess up, just repeat it."

"Okay." I took a breath while she closed the soundproof door. Then I read, "Wendy Newman begins her day at six in the morning and has to be at the sports arena by seven-thirty." I looked up.

Lauren nodded and gave me a hand signal that meant keep going.

"Exercise is the first routine of the day. Wendy's warm-up is led by her personal trainer, Gabriel Smith. After half an hour I was too tired to go on, but Wendy still had another fifteen minutes left. I don't know how she does it."

I finished reading about twenty minutes later, and when I got back downstairs, Kathleen was already in our dressing room. She was still in her burgundy-and-white school uniform doing her homework on the sofa.

She didn't look up when I entered, and for a few minutes we didn't speak. I didn't know what to say to her. If I apologized she would think I was feeling sorry for her.

So instead I said, "How's your mother?"

She didn't take her eyes off her books. "What do you care?"

"You could have told me the truth, you know. I'm not a baby. I would have understood."

"What would you know about this? You have a perfect mother."

"I do not," I said. "And that's not the point. From the first day on, all you've done is lie to me, tease me, and try to boss me around. Let's face it, you never tried to be friends with me."

"You didn't exactly bend over backward to be mine," she said, looking up at me. "You acted pretty high and mighty yourself. After all, you made it very clear that you were the one with all the experience on the show."

There was a knock at the door. Penny poked her head in. "Is everything okay in here?" We nodded, and she came into the room carrying several hangers of clothes. She hung them on a rack and separated Kathleen's from mine. "Try these on, girls. You each will have three wardrobe changes."

When she left, Kathleen and I reached for our clothes in silence. I tried on a pair of yellow shorts first and they fit okay. Then I tried on a green dress that had a long zipper up the back. "Can you zip me, Kathleen?" I asked, half expecting her to tell me to buzz off.

But she didn't. She zipped me up and asked me to turn around so she could see how it looked. "That's the ugliest dress I've ever seen," she said, giggling. "If I were you I'd *beg* Penny to give me something else."

I looked in the mirror. "It is pretty bad, isn't it?"

In the reflection I saw her nod. She unzipped my dress and I stepped out of it. As I hung it up she said, "About my mother. I think she's going to be okay."

"Great. That must be a relief."

"It is. I'm glad she finally admitted she needs help, that she can't stop drinking on her own."

I took the next outfit off the hanger thinking about the drunk driver who ran into Dad's car. If she had gotten help, my father would still be alive. "What about your father?" I asked.

"My parents were divorced when I was a baby. Since then my mother has been married and divorced two more times. I haven't see my father in years." She took a deep breath. "Things have been really hard on my mother. She hasn't made a movie in about five years, and she had to raise Jeanette and me by herself."

For the first time since we met, I felt sorry for Kathleen. I don't know how I would react if Mom drank. "Is there anything I can do?" I asked.

She nodded. "You can go see Penny and get on your hands and knees, that's what you can do. I just can't have that dress on *my* show."

This time she was only kidding. I guess that was her way of saying everything was okay.

· · · · · · ·

The moment Mrs. Hoffman walked into our classroom the next day she told us to clear off our desks. Kelly and I looked at each other in amazement. No teacher would give a surprise quiz on the second day of school.

"Class, you have fifteen minutes to complete this quiz. It's on the work we covered yesterday."

Before the papers reached us, Kelly whispered, "Did you study?"

"I barely had time to do the homework," I said.

The quiz had a little of everything. Questions on history, math, and science. Then we had to match words with their definitions. Needless to say, I didn't know anything.

Afterward, while we worked in our math workbooks, Mrs. Hoffman corrected our papers at her desk. This is going to be a tough year, I thought. Never in my life had I been so lost on a quiz.

Right before lunch, Mrs. Hoffman handed back the papers, announcing each grade aloud. I got seventy-one, the lowest grade in the class. I wanted to die of embarrassment.

Then, to top things off, Mrs. Hoffman called me to her desk while everybody left for the lunchroom. "What happened?" she asked me.

I looked down at the floor. "I don't know."

"Delaney, you're going to have to study every single night. I'm known for my surprise quizzes."

Just my luck.

"From now on I'm going to assign plenty of homework. Try to stay on top of things, okay?"

"Okay."

She smiled. "And don't worry too much about this quiz. If you work hard, you can make up for it."

• • • • • • •

Bryce and I went to see Grendel after school again. While we were there the owner of The Lily Pad asked us if we wanted to feed him.

"What does he eat?" I asked.

Bryce smiled devilishly. "White mice."

"Ugh!"

"You two want to feed him?" the man repeated.

Bryce said yes and I said no at the exact same time. Then we looked at each other.

I put my hands on my hips. "I'm not going to watch that thing eat a mouse, Bryce. Come on and take me to work." Again I had to literally pull him out of the store.

As we walked along the street I asked Bryce what he thought about his father and my mother dating.

"Honestly?" he asked.

"Of course."

"Honestly, I think it's . . ." He made a face as though he were searching for the right word. "Well, let me put it like this. At first I thought it was strange, but now I think it's cool."

"Why did you think it was strange?"

"Well, I never thought my dad would date a black woman. It surprised me."

"And why do you think it's cool now?"

"Because I got to know your mother and I like her. My dad used to mope around every Friday night, but now he's changed. He even whistles before he goes to work."

Times Square was busy as usual, with cars coming from every direction. We made it to the middle of the street, then had to wait as a never-ending stream of cars whisked in front of us. When there was a slight break Bryce grabbed my hand and ran with me the rest of the way.

"Tell me what you think about them," he said on our way into the network building.

"I'm not sure," I said. "It never crossed my mind that my mom would date anyone. When she told me that she liked your dad I felt funny about it at first. I didn't want people to talk about her behind her back."

"I thought about that, too."

"But I don't care about that anymore. There are people who always find something to talk about. But don't you think the two of them spend too much time together? Sometimes I wish it were still just Mom and me."

Bryce pressed for the elevator. "When you get older you're not going to want to be around your mother all the time. You're going to have parties to go to and club meetings at school. And what about when you go away to college? Your mother is going to be lonely."

I hadn't thought of that before.

"I'm glad my father's dating now," he said. "He talks about your mother all the time, and he's real happy. That's all that matters."

The elevator came, and I had to wave good-bye to Bryce because he didn't have the proper identification to go upstairs. "Thanks for picking me up," I said. "And talking to me."

He smiled. "Have a good rehearsal."

When the doors closed I leaned against the back wall, glad nobody else was in there. I had never seen that side of Bryce before, but I liked it.

· · · · · · ·

When Mom came to pick me up at seven o'clock, Lauren wasn't finished with us yet.

She had given us the show rundown for the first show and wanted to go over it before we left. "As you can see," Lauren said, "the show is packed with different things. We have the segment from Letchworth State Park, Kathleen's fashion show, Cory's new segment, Delaney's piece on Wendy Newman, the review of *Class Secrets*, the Billy Denim interview, and Kathleen's Listen Up! segment. That's quite a lot to fit into one hour. So remember to keep the energy level up at all times so the show doesn't drag."

Mom waited in the back of the studio with Cory's parents, glancing at her watch every few minutes. I could tell that she wanted us to get going, but Lauren had more things she wanted to say to us.

Finally Mom came over to me and whispered, "Honey, go get your knapsack."

"We're not finished yet," I said. Everyone was staring at us.

"It's almost eight o'clock. You're done for the day."

I stood up hesitantly. Why was Mom doing this? I looked at Lauren.

"I apologize, kids," she said. "I didn't realize it was so late. We'll continue tomorrow morning."

In the cab Mom was still angry. "Who does Lauren think she's working with? Doesn't she understand that children cannot stay out all night when they have school the next day?"

I leaned against her shoulder, exhausted.

"I'm going to have a talk with Ms. Seachman tomorrow," she continued. "She's going to have to do something about this schedule."

Mom was already so upset. It wouldn't be right to bring up that horrible quiz grade.

At home I wanted to go right to sleep, but I still had

homework to do. And studying. I had to be prepared for any more surprise quizzes.

After changing into my pajamas, I lay on my bed with my computer textbook open to the first chapter. It was nine pages long, with only two drawings that didn't take up much space.

I drifted off to sleep somewhere between byte and ROM.

15

· ·

I had to be at the studio at six-thirty the next morning. We had breakfast, then spent a couple of hours running through the opening of the show until we felt comfortable and it looked casual. As Lauren put it, we had to rehearse looking unrehearsed.

"Let's try it again from the top," Lauren said.

The three of us were sitting on the miniature staircase where we would begin the show on Friday.

"Okay, action."

Kathleen smiled. "Hi. Welcome to 'Friday Afternoon.' I'm Kathleen."

"Boring," Lauren interrupted. "Loosen up."

Kathleen put her head down on her lap. "This would be so much easier if we had a script."

I had to agree with her. Every other time I had done television work, there was always a script to work from. But here we were on our own.

Lauren said, "For the opening all you have to do is

introduce yourselves and tell the viewers what's coming up on the show. You don't need a script for that. I want your personalities to shine through."

Ms. Seachman came into the studio. "Delaney, you'd better get going now."

I glanced at my watch. It was almost nine o'clock. "Oh no! I'm late for school."

Lauren quickly wrapped up what she was doing and told all of us to get to school. Kathleen and Cory didn't have to be at Saxon until ten, but I was supposed to be at my school at eight-thirty.

"You're late, Miss Crawford," the principal, Mrs. Alvarez, said the second I walked into her office for a late pass.

"I know. I had rehearsal and we lost track of time."

"That's no excuse." She wrote out the pass and handed me the slip of paper. "This had better be the last time."

• • • • • • •

We didn't have rehearsal that afternoon. We met at the studio, then went uptown to see a private screening of a movie that was going to be released on Friday. It was a teenage movie, so Kathleen and Cory enjoyed it more than I did. It was really funny, though.

That evening I decided to write my review while the movie was still fresh in my mind. Lauren said we should try to find both good and bad things to say about it, and we shouldn't reveal too much of the plot to the audience.

After I was done, I began my homework. I had math, social studies, and some reading to do in my computer text. When I opened my math workbook I shook my head. I didn't understand a thing because Mrs. Hoffman had taught math first thing in the morning, before I arrived.

"Mrs. Alvarez called my office this morning to chew me out," Mom told me over dinner. "I felt like a child who had been called to the principal's office."

"It wasn't your fault I was late. She just likes to yell."

"Then I called Ms. Seachman. She told me to reconsider the Saxon School."

"But I don't want to go there."

"How are you doing in class? Are you keeping up?"

I thought about the math I didn't know how to do, and all the other homework I wouldn't get to tonight. "Yeah," I said. "I'm doing okay." I looked down at my food so she couldn't tell I was lying. But I was starting to panic inside. There just wasn't enough time in the day to do everything.

· · · · · · ·

It was seven-thirty the next morning, and we had been at the studio since six o'clock. Makeup. Wardrobe. Rehearsal. And now we were out in Central Park shooting the opening to the show. We had put this off for a few days because it hadn't been sunny enough, so it was now or never.

"We have forty-five minutes," Lauren told us. "So there's no time to fool around. Does everyone know what to do?"

"Yes," we all chorused.

"Good, then take your places."

We were shooting several short clips of us playing Frisbee on the Great Lawn that would be shown while the "Friday Afternoon" theme music played.

Forty-five minutes wasn't a lot of time, and I began to

feel bad that I was putting pressure on the cast and crew. It wasn't really fair to them. Even though nobody said anything, I knew I was making things a little harder.

Fortunately, I got to school on time. Unfortunately, I still had on makeup. I hadn't realized it until I walked into my classroom and everyone stared at me.

"I see Delaney is celebrating Halloween early," Mrs. Hoffman said.

"Huh?" I touched my cheek and saw the powdered blush on my fingertips. "On no. I was in such a rush to get here on time, I forgot about this junk."

Everyone laughed. The makeup was very heavy and scary looking off camera. Halloween was right!

"You have five minutes to scrub your face, Delaney," Mrs. Hoffman said. "Five minutes."

When I returned to the classroom ten minutes later, Mrs. Hoffman had written some math problems on the blackboard. She clapped her hands together. "Okay, I need some people to work out these problems on the board. Any volunteers?"

Kelly and a few other kids raised their hands. Mrs. Hoffman had noticed when I returned because she said, "You don't tell time very well, Delaney. Maybe you'll have better luck at the board."

The problems involved adding mixed fractions, and I really didn't remember being taught how to do them. I just stood at the board staring at the problem as if the answer would magically come to me.

Kelly whispered to me, "Find the least-common denominator."

"No talking," Mrs. Hoffman said loudly. "Let Delaney do her own work."

I picked up the chalk to make it look as if I was trying, but after everyone had sat down I was still standing there, completely embarrassed.

"Have you studied, Delaney?" Mrs. Hoffman asked.

I shook my head.

She coached me through the problem until I came up with the right answer. Everyone in the whole class was looking at me, and I felt incredibly stupid. Tears stung my eyes and got caught in my lashes. I had to blink them away fast. There was no way I could let the class see me cry.

· · · · · · ·

I ran into Tasha in the bathroom after lunch. She was standing at the mirror combing her hair. At first we both just looked at each other. I didn't want to say hello if she wouldn't say it back. And then I thought, Why do I always have to be the one to make up? She could talk to me just as easily.

So I didn't say anything. I went into one of the stalls. When I came out Gina Foster was there. The two of them were whispering. I heard Gina say, "Congratulations! How do you feel?"

Tasha laughed. "I don't know. I feel a little different, I guess."

I soaped up my hands angrily and rinsed them off. Who did she think she was?

"Well, you should. You're a woman now." Gina gave her a kiss on the cheek. "I have to go. I'm meeting Greg on the staircase."

When she left I couldn't hold my tongue any longer.

"You promised that I would be the first person you'd tell," I said a little too loudly.

"We were friends when I made that promise. It doesn't count anymore." She shrugged her shoulders matter-of-factly.

I pulled off a piece of brown paper towel from the dispenser. "A promise is a promise," I said, drying my hands.

"I don't see what difference it makes. I got my period last night. We both knew I'd get it before you anyway." She leaned closer to the mirror and put on lip gloss. When did she start wearing that?

"You think you're perfect, don't you?" I asked.

"Delaney, stop acting juvenile."

I didn't want to listen to her. "Let's see. You have the perfect face, the perfect figure, and the perfect father. How does it feel?"

Tasha looked at me as if it were the first time she was seeing me. "What are you talking about?"

"Oh, pardon me. I must be acting juvenile again!" I left the bathroom without saying another word.

· · · · · · ·

All afternoon I could barely concentrate on what Mrs. Hoffman was saying. Not only was I totally embarrassed about what I had said to Tasha, I was also exhausted. I had gotten up at four-thirty that morning, and I still had a long day ahead of me.

Mrs. Hoffman came over and stood by my desk. "Am I keeping you awake, Delaney?" she asked sarcastically.

I looked up. "Huh? Oh, no."

"Good, then why don't you repeat what I was just telling the class?"

I looked around. Behind Mrs. Hoffman's back, Malik Rashid held up our computer textbook. "Um, you were talking about computers," I said. Malik shuffled through some papers and held up the quiz we had taken on Tuesday. "We're having a computer quiz."

Mrs. Hoffman nodded. "Well done. You and Malik work together like pros."

How did she do that?

"The quiz tomorrow will be on chapters one and two," she told the class. "If you have been keeping up with your reading assignments, this should be no problem at all."

I knew what that meant. I was in deep trouble.

· · · · · · · ·

That afternoon we had technical rehearsal, which is just about the most boring thing in the world. Kathleen, Cory, and I had to run through the show segment by segment and wait as Mike and the crew got the lighting straight and figured out the proper camera shots. It took a looong time.

When the attention shifted to Cory's news segment, Lauren told Kathleen and me to go to our dressing room and have dinner. The two of us sat on the floor on either side of the coffee table, too drained to talk. I was still thinking about Tasha, and school, and what a mess I was making of everything.

Lauren knocked on the door several minutes later. "Kathleen, Mike needs you on the set now."

Kathleen shoved another piece of pepper steak in her mouth and jumped up. When she had gone Lauren came in and sat next to me. "You seem far away this evening," she said. "We have a few minutes before Mike will need you. My offer still holds."

"What offer?"

"Remember I said if you ever had a problem you could talk to me."

"I thought you were just being nice."

"I'm listening," she said.

I shrugged. "Okay, but you asked for it." I quickly told her about how Tasha and I hadn't been speaking all summer, about our arguments, and about what I had said to her in the bathroom that afternoon.

For a while Lauren was silent. Then she said, "Looks like your jealousy is back."

"Jealousy?" I looked down. "I'm not jealous of Tasha. It's just that she has everything. . . . Everything that I don't have."

"Sounds like jealousy to me."

Tears filled my eyes instantly. "I tried to make up with her the night I slept over at her house, but she didn't want to. Now she's trying to take Kelly's friendship away from me."

Lauren gave me a funny look, as if I was being ridiculous.

I sighed. There was no way to explain it all. Lauren just didn't understand.

Then she asked me how I was doing in school.

I decided to come clean. "Not too good. I'm beginning to think it's not fair for me to keep going to my school. I know I'm causing a lot of trouble for you and everyone else on the show."

"Don't worry about what's fair for us, Delaney. You have to decide what's fair for you."

· · · · · · ·

By the time I got home that evening I had a killer head-ache. There was so much on my mind and it was all getting to me. I really didn't need that kind of pressure. Not with the show starting tomorrow.

Mom took me into her bedroom and told me to sit on the floor with my legs folded and eyes closed. Then she knelt behind me and slowly rubbed her fingers on my temples. "Relax your body and clear your mind."

"I can't," I cried. My head felt like it was bursting at the seams.

"Okay, then think about what's bothering you. But take your time with it. And try to stop crying."

I nodded. That's what I had to do. Think about it.

"I want you to count down from ten very slowly while you relax all of your muscles," Mom said in a soothing tone. "Then imagine you're in a dark tunnel and you're completely weightless, like in outer space."

I let my arms and back go limp as the heat from Mom's hands sank into my head. Pictures of Tasha and Kelly flashed through my mind. I had to solve this problem, not to mention the school situation.

I began to feel myself slip away into the darkness. And before I knew it, I did feel like I was floating through a tunnel. I didn't have any problems at that moment. It was great.

After a while I began to think about everything that had happened over the summer. It felt strange that Kelly and Tasha were close friends now. And that they shared things that didn't include me. Lauren was right. It was just my stupid jealousy getting in the way again.

After all, Kelly and I shared things that we didn't share with Tasha. Like her puberty book, cooking, and our friendship bracelets. Tasha couldn't change that.

And who knows? Maybe even Tasha and I would make up. She wasn't trying to take my place with Kelly. She just wanted a friend as much as I did.

After several minutes I opened my eyes. "It's gone. My headache's gone."

Mom stopped rubbing my head. "Are you sure?"

"Yeah! That meditation thing really works." I stood up. "I feel terrific now."

"Do you want to lie in my bed tonight?" she asked, turning down her covers. "I'm very concerned about you."

"I'm fine," I said. "But I've come to a decision about school. I'm going to the Saxon School if that's okay with you."

"If you think it'll be better."

"It will. Not only for me, but for Lauren and Kathleen and Cory, too. I've been selfish."

"Okay, I'll call the school first thing in the morning." Mom kissed me good night. "I'm very proud of you for making this decision on your own. Sometimes we have to give up a lot for the things we want."

"But like I said before, it's worth it. I'll miss going to school with my friends, but it's not like I'll never see them again."

Honestly, I was glad I had made this decision on my own, too. It proved that I didn't have to run to Mom every time I had a problem. Maybe I *was* growing up.

16

I jumped out of bed the next morning, nervous and excited. The first show was today! I ran into the kitchen
where Mom was making breakfast. "Did Lauren call yet?"
I asked. "What time do I have to be there? Did you call
the school?"

"Calm down," Mom said, laughing. "Lauren called and
she wants us all to have lunch together at noon. And we
have a ten-thirty appointment at the Saxon School."

It was only eight o'clock now.

"Sit down and have something to eat," Mom said.

"I couldn't possibly eat anything. Not now. I'm too
nervous." I went back into my room and crawled into
bed. The photograph on the wall caught my eye. I wondered if Dad would think I was taking the easy way out
by going to the Saxon School.

Mom came in a few minutes later with a glass of milk.
She saw me looking at the picture. "Your father loved
you very much, Delaney," she said, sitting on my bed and

handing me the glass. "But not because you're an actress. He loved you because you're a very special person."

I sipped the milk and said, "I just want to make him proud, that's all."

"Is that why you've put so much pressure on yourself?" I could tell she was still worried about my headaches.

I shrugged. "A little. I'm glad Dad got me started in television, but I wouldn't continue to do something I didn't like. And I love performing, Mom. I really do."

Mom stood up. "Hurry up and get dressed. We have to stop by your old school and pick up your records."

"My old school?" I hadn't thought of that, but I guess it was my old school.

"Come on, don't get sad, Delaney. Not today." She kissed me on the forehead. "This is your special day, one you've worked very hard for. I don't want you to spoil it by worrying unnecessarily."

"But—"

"Remember, I only signed a one-year contract with the show, Delaney. Next summer you'll decide if you want to do another year. If you don't, you can join your friends in junior high school."

I smiled. Why hadn't I thought of that before? "Thanks, Mom. And you're right. Nothing is going to spoil this day for me."

· · · · · · ·

While Mom picked up my records from the office, I went down the hall to my classroom to return my textbooks. Everyone looked at me when I walked in. "Do you have a late pass?" Mrs. Hoffman asked me. "And how come you're not in uniform?"

I dropped the books on her desk. "Um, I just came to return my books. I'm changing schools."

Mrs. Hoffman told the class to continue doing the work on the board. Converting fractions to decimals. Ugh! While she checked the books, I looked at Kelly, who was already staring at me. I didn't know what to say to her, so I kind of shrugged. She looked sad, and I felt like a total rat for deserting her.

"What school are you going to?" Mrs. Hoffman asked me.

"The Saxon School for Professional Children."

"That's a fine school. I wish you the very best."

"Thank you."

Before I left everyone wished me luck on the show and told me they'd be watching. Kelly stood up and gave me a long hug. "I'm going to miss being in class with you," she whispered. "Good luck this afternoon."

In front of the whole class I couldn't tell her that I finally realized that our friendship was unique and that it no longer bothered me that she and Tasha were good friends. I also couldn't ask her if she would help me make up with Tasha. So after our hug I just said, "Thanks."

Walking back down the empty hallway it hit me. This wasn't my school anymore. I'd never be here again.

· · · · · · ·

The Saxon School was in a small building located just three blocks from the network building. When we got inside, Mom and I became very impressed. The hallway was carpeted, and the walls were covered with several photographs of the students in different costumes. It seemed like most of the kids were in Broadway plays and musicals.

We spent about a half hour talking to the principal, Mr. Appleton. Mom asked a zillion questions about the school while I sat quietly listening. I wondered if I'd make any friends at this school.

"We get a lot of work done here in four hours," Mr. Appleton told Mom. "And we will work very closely with her tutor. She will be doing the same work as children in every other sixth-grade class."

After Mom filled out the registration forms and ordered Saxon School uniforms for me, Mr. Appleton took us on a minitour of the building. There was only one classroom for each grade, each with no more than ten students in it.

Mom waited in the hallway as he took me into the sixth-grade class and introduced me to the teacher, Mr. Bennett. I had never had a man for a teacher before, but he seemed nice.

I looked around nervously. The room was nicely decorated. All the students' desks were arranged in a semicircle and everyone was busy working. There were ten math problems on the blackboard. Converting fractions to decimals. Ugh! There was no getting out of it.

Mr. Appleton asked for attention. "Class, we have a new student. I'm sure you'll all welcome Delaney Crawford to Saxon."

Talk about feeling awkward! I looked up and tried to smile, hoping to appear friendly. Starting Monday, these would be my classmates.

Everyone in the class said hi to me, and Mr. Bennett told me that he'd be glad to have me in his class. As Mom and I walked down the hallway toward the front entrance, she put her arm around my shoulder. "This is a very lovely school. I'm sure you'll make friends right away."

I was going to say something, but one of the photographs caught my attention. It was a picture of Wendy Newman in a beautiful white skating outfit with a gold medal around her neck and flowers in her hands.

"That's Wendy," I told Mom. "The girl I interviewed. I didn't know she went to this school." Wendy and I were both eleven years old. We'd be in the same class!

In the taxi on the way to the studio I became really excited about the show. In a little over four hours we'd be on television for the whole country to see. And even though I hadn't seen how all the segments turned out, I was pretty sure the show would be a lot of fun.

When we got off the elevator on the seventeenth floor, Cory was standing in the hallway with his parents. "What am I going to do?" he asked.

Mrs. Drennen looked closely at his face. "It's just a little blemish, dear."

"It's not a *little* anything, Mom. It's a big, fat, ugly zit! My life is over." He ran to his dressing room, saying, "I knew this would happen."

Mom and I looked at each other and shrugged. Then we went to Lauren's office to tell her that I had transferred to the Saxon School.

She looked relieved. "I think you made the right decision, Delaney," she said. Then she wrote out a new rehearsal schedule for me. I had to work from seven-thirty to nine-thirty in the morning, go to school from ten to two, then work again from two-thirty to four-thirty.

It was perfect. There wouldn't be any more late hours at the studio. I could visit Kelly and Tasha before dinner and still have time to study.

"This schedule won't apply on Fridays or the days you tape your segment," Lauren said. "On those days you'll be tutored only."

I could tell that Mom was still worried about what kind of education I'd get, but she took the paper and said it sounded okay with her. In the hallway I told her, "I'll study real hard, Mom. And I promise to tell you if I'm having trouble this time."

She hugged me. "Oh, honey. I just want you to have the best of everything."

I hugged her tighter. "I already do."

· · · · · · ·

We all went to lunch together at the same restaurant Lauren and I had gone to for our business lunch. There were ten of us all together: Lauren, Eric, Mike, Cory and his parents, Kathleen and her sister, Jeanette, and Mom and me. We'd reserved a private room and had a great time even though Lauren kept reminding us that we had to be back at the studio by one-thirty.

Before we left the restaurant Lauren asked us all to hold up our water glasses for the toast. "To the success of 'Friday Afternoon,' " she said.

We all responded, "Hear, hear!" Kathleen, Cory, and I clinked glasses so hard that water spilled down our hands and arms. We laughed and clinked again, harder. This time Cory's glass cracked.

"A broken glass is good luck," Kathleen said. "I read that somewhere."

We knew she had just made that up, but who cared? We needed all the luck we could get.

"Are you nervous?" Kathleen asked me an hour before air time. We were already made up, and our hair was styled for the first segment.

"A little," I said, waving my hands around so the nail polish could finish drying. "What about you?"

"Kind of."

I sat on the love seat next to Mom and looked at some silly show on television. Someone had put a set in our dressing room so we could watch the show while we were changing clothes. Actually, I was more nervous than I had let on, but I didn't want Kathleen to get scared just because I was.

There was a knock on the dressing room door. Jeanette opened it a crack, since Kathleen and I were walking around in only our bathrobes. "Delaney, it's your agent," she said.

Mom stood up and said, "I'll talk to him until you finish dressing."

Ten minutes later one of Lauren's assistants, CJ, came into the room to help us get ready. My first outfit was the yellow shorts with a blue T-shirt. We were all dressed casually for the first segment because we were supposed to look as if we'd just come home from school and changed into play clothes.

"You have to take this off," CJ said, referring to my friendship bracelet.

"Why can't I wear it? It matches."

"Penny said you can't wear anything that isn't on the list."

"Please, CJ. I want my best friend to see me with it on TV."

She sighed. "I'll go see what Penny says."

When she left, I paced back and forth hoping Penny would say yes. The bracelet meant a lot to me. And I had promised Kelly I would never take it off.

"I don't think Penny will go for it," Kathleen said as her sister did the buttons on the back of her one-piece shorts outfit. "Remember what happened when you asked if she'd exchange the ugly green dress."

"Oh, yeah." Penny had said no before I'd even finished asking. She said wardrobe wasn't up for discussion. What she said went!

When CJ came back she said, "You're one lucky girl, Delaney. Penny said all right."

I fingered the small beads on my wrist. "Thanks. I know Kelly will be happy to see me wearing it."

When I was finished dressing, I went out to the hallway to say hello to Mr. Kirby. He was wearing a green polo shirt with blue pants. "For you," he said, giving me a huge stuffed giraffe. The bow around its neck had "Good Luck" printed all over it.

"Thanks! He's adorable. Are you staying for the whole show?"

"I wouldn't miss it."

Lauren flew down the hallway. As she passed us she said, "Thirty minutes, Delaney. Tell the others."

I turned to Mom, panic stricken. "Did she just say—"

"Now don't get nervous," Mom said. "I don't want you to get another headache." Then she told Mr. Kirby about all the pressure I had been under and about the bad headache I had had last night.

"I'll be right back," I said, and ran to Cory's dressing room. He opened the door. "Thirty minutes," I said.

His eyes opened wide. "For real?"

I nodded and went down to my dressing room. When I told Kathleen she freaked out. "Oh my goodness! I'm not ready yet."

"Me neither," I said, placing the giraffe on my love seat. He looked cute and gave the dressing room a comfortable feel. But I wasn't feeling all that comfortable. I was a wreck.

Soon both Kathleen and I were pacing around the dressing room.

"Would you two relax," Jeanette said. "You're just making yourselves more nervous."

I sat down on the love seat, then bounced up again. How could I relax when I'd be on television in less than a half hour? A little while later Mom came into the dressing room. "Lauren told me to tell you it's twenty minutes before air time."

"Oh no!" I shouted, and grabbed my head. I could feel a headache coming on. Then I looked up. "Mom, show me how to meditate again."

"Me too," Kathleen said.

"Let's go in the rehearsal room," I said. "Then Cory can meditate with us."

When all three of us were in the rehearsal room with our legs folded, Mom told us to take a deep cleansing breath.

Cory laughed. "What's that mean?"

"Close your eyes," Mom said. "And breathe in deeply. When you let it go I want you to feel all the pressure and nervousness go out with it. Do that five times."

We all did what she said, and honestly it did make me

feel a little better. Then Mom told us to do the same thing I had done last night. This time while I was in the tunnel I imagined Kathleen and Cory with me and we were all happy. The way I hoped we'd be after the show was over.

When we finished meditating we were all smiling. Lauren poked her head in the door. "Come into the studio now, troops."

We held hands as we walked down the hallway. After all the talk about being a team, it wasn't until that very moment that we felt like one.

· · · · · · ·

"Five minutes," someone announced. The studio was bustling with activity. Ms. Seachman and all of the associate producers were talking in the back of the room. People I had never seen before were hurrying around passing papers to other people I had never seen. Lauren was making last-minute preparations with the stage manager, Jim.

I looked around completely lost. The hair stylist went from Kathleen to me to Cory, putting the finishing touches on us. A big television monitor off to one side of the room showed all the studio commotion, but pretty soon it would be showing the real thing.

Kathleen, Cory, and I were sitting on the staircase underneath the "Friday Afternoon" sign, burning up under the hot lights. Ms. Seachman walked over to us. "How are you three doing?"

None of us said anything. We all just nodded.

Mom and Mr. Kirby came into the studio and stood in the back of the room. She gave me a thumbs-up sign and smiled.

More commotion. More people running around.

"Two minutes!"

"Oh my goodness," Kathleen said. She looked terrified.

Something had to be done. We were falling apart again. "There's no reason to be nervous," I said to Kathleen and Cory.

They looked at me. "Easy for you to say," Cory said. Then he looked around the room, his face gone completely white. "What am I doing here?"

"Cory, pull yourself together," I said. "Come on. We can do this if we relax. Remember what my mother taught us. It works."

Kathleen nodded and took a deep cleansing breath. "That feels good."

Then we all did it. I tried to imagine I was in my bedroom doing the show in front of my mirror. There were no cameras or lights. Nobody was around. It was just me and—

"One minute!"

My eyes popped open. "Did he just say one minute!"

Cory nodded. "Let's huddle."

We stood up on the steps and wrapped our arms around each other's back until we were in a small circle. "Are we going to have fun?" I asked.

Kathleen giggled. "This is what we worked all summer for. If we don't have fun, something's wrong with us!"

Mike's voice came over the speaker system. "Okay, take your places."

Both Kathleen and I sat on the top stair, and Cory sat one step below us. We clipped our microphones to our clothes and waited. Within seconds all the other people had dashed from the set. Lauren stood behind the cameras off to one side, looking worried.

"This is it, kids," Jim said, coming out to the center of the room. "Good luck. We're going live in five, four, three, two . . ." He held up one finger as the theme music began to play.

17

On the television monitor the clips of us playing Frisbee in Central Park accompanied the theme music, and after about ten seconds the words "Friday Afternoon" appeared on the screen in the same fancy lettering as the sign behind us. Kathleen and I looked at each other. This was it!

When I looked at the monitor again there was a shot of the three of us sitting on the staircase. I can't explain what I was feeling. It was really exciting to be on television after so many weeks of preparing and rehearsing, but there was also a heavy feeling in the pit of my stomach. And I knew that wouldn't go away until the show was over.

When the music faded, that was our cue to begin. Kathleen put on one of her model's smiles and said, "Hi, I'm Kathleen."

"I'm Cory."

I smiled, too. "And I'm Delaney."

Then Kathleen and I chorused together. "And it's 'Friday Afternoon'!"

Cory turned around and looked up at us. "We all know it's Friday afternoon, girls. I mean we went to school five days in a row and—"

" 'Friday Afternoon' is the name of our show, silly," I said.

Then Kathleen said, "Let's tell everyone what's coming up on the show."

"Okay," Cory said. "We'll be showing highlights from our fossil dig in upstate New York and reviewing *Class Secrets*, a new movie that opens today in theaters all across the country."

Kathleen perked up. "And don't forget our exclusive interview with Billy Denim—"

"Or your fashion show, Kathleen," Cory added. "And what about your feature on the junior champion figure skater, Delaney?"

I smiled. "And I'm sure you have a lot of interesting things for your news segment."

Kathleen said, "But first, here's Billy Denim's video 'Don't Even Start.' Enjoy it!"

We looked into the monitor until it showed Billy on stage dancing around in that unique way of his. Then we all took a few of those deep cleansing breaths Mom had taught us. The video was about four and a half minutes long. Then we would be back on the air.

Ms. Seachman and Lauren came over to us.

"I bit my tongue," Kathleen said. "I think it's bleeding."

Ms. Seachman looked at it. "No, there's no blood."

"You're doing very well so far," Lauren said. "The energy is great, but don't get so excited that you cut each other off. After the video is over, all you have to do is take us into the first commercial break. We've gone over it a few times. Do you have any questions?"

We shook our heads.

The four and a half minutes went by very quickly. As we heard Billy Denim singing his last chorus, Lauren checked to see that our microphones were still attached properly.

When the video ended and we were back on the air, I said, "That was terrific!"

"Billy Denim is a master at the guitar," Cory said.

"Not to mention a mega hunk," Kathleen added.

Both Cory and I looked at her. We didn't think she would say something like that on television.

She laughed. "We'll be right back after these commercial messages with highlights from our trip to Letchworth State Park. Stay with us."

The theme music played again, and we watched the monitor until it blacked out and we knew we were off the air. I felt so relieved at that moment. We had made it to the first commerical, and we were still alive.

During the break CJ brought us little bottles of spring water. Then we moved over to the middle set, the three director-style chairs in front of the video screens. CJ helped me get into my tall chair and attached all our microphones for us.

"Twenty seconds," Jim announced.

"Are we still having fun?" I whispered to Kathleen and Cory.

"Ask me that when it's over," Cory said.

Jim came out to the center of the floor again. "Okay, kids. We're going live again in five, four, three, two . . ."

The theme music played again, but only for a few seconds. Then Cory said, "Welcome back to 'Friday Afternoon.' Last weekend we all went upstate on a geology dig. Here's what happened."

And that took us into the videotaped footage from our trip. We all got up to stretch our legs. This was a long segment.

"This is easy," I said to Kathleen. "We've done most of the work already. All we have to do now is set up the clips."

"It's not so easy for Cory and me," she said. "We have to do our segments live."

"Oh, yeah," I said. Cory's news piece was coming up in a little while, and Kathleen had to go down on the street and do her Listen Up! segment near the end of the show.

I walked around the studio trying to figure out how I would introduce the next commercial. It was my turn. "Cory," I said, going over to where he was standing with his parents. "How does this sound: 'We'll be right back with Kathleen's fall fashion show and Bits and Pieces from Cory.' "

"Good," he said. "It's simple and to the point."

"Thanks." I walked away repeating it over and over so I wouldn't forget it.

"Take your places," Mike said over the loudspeaker. "We have one minute."

As I struggled to get back into my tall director's chair, a bulb on one side of the studio blew. A weird shadow crossed our faces.

"Can someone change the bulb?" Mike asked impatiently. "We're on the air in forty seconds."

Then out of nowhere one of the crew members ran over with a tall ladder and a huge light bulb in his hand. We were all watching him, wondering if he could possibly climb up there and change it in half a minute.

He reached the top and had difficulty unscrewing the old bulb. I pounded my fists on my lap anxiously. The show had been going so great until now, and I didn't want anything to spoil it.

Jim counted down. "Five, four . . ."

The light flicked on and we all breathed sighs of relief. "Three, two . . ."

We only had two minutes until the second commercial break, so the three of us had a brief discussion about the trip. We all agreed that it was fun, even in the miserable weather.

Kathleen said, "There are several groups across the country that sponsor weekend digs for kids and teenagers. So, if you're interested, get a paper and pen and we'll print up some phone numbers later in the show."

Then there was a close-up of me. It was time for me to introduce the commercial. I smiled into the camera and said, "We'll be back after this commercial with . . ." Suddenly I couldn't remember what was coming up next. My mind was blank. I took a quick breath and said, "With more of 'Friday Afternoon.' "

As the music played and the monitors blacked out, I felt like a total jerk. How could I forget one stupid line? What was the matter with me? Kathleen and Cory dashed into their dressing rooms for their quick wardrobe change, but I had time since I wasn't in the next two segments.

I went to the back of the studio with my head held low.

"Don't worry about it, Delaney," Mom said. "Nobody knows what you were supposed to say. You sounded just fine."

I looked over at Lauren, and she winked at me.

As Kathleen flew into the studio dressed in a pretty red dress, Mom and I left and went back to my dressing room. We turned on the television set and watched as Kathleen introduced the video clip of her fashion show. Then she came back into the dressing room and we watched it together. There had been seven models, four girls and three boys, and the clothes were perfect for both school and weekends.

Then there was Cory's Bits & Pieces segment. I didn't get a chance to see the whole thing, but what I did see was good. He was reporting fun news, not the kind of thing you see at six o'clock. Most of what he was talking about had to do with kids doing wacky stuff all over the country.

The reason I couldn't sit down and watch it was because I had to get dressed to introduce my Wendy Newman piece. CJ came in to help me into my ugly green dress, but when she tried to zip up the back, it got stuck.

"What am I going to do?" I asked her, anxiously. I had less than two minutes to get out there.

"Take it off," CJ said. "I'll go down and see if Penny has anything else."

When she left Kathleen said, "Look on the bright side. At least you don't have to wear that thing."

Yeah! Things worked out after all.

CJ came back with a pale pink dress with a white belt. It was a little big for me, but it wasn't that bad.

"Knock them dead," Mom said before I ran down to the studio.

I was alone in front of the camera this time, but I wasn't nervous. I sat on the bottom stair and casually said, "Last week I spent the day with Wendy Newman, the current junior world champion figure skater. It is the first of my weekly series."

On the monitor I saw a close-up picture of one of the twelve video screens. In fancy writing it said, "A Day in the Life of a Figure Skater." Then it went right into the videotape of me going up the walk to Wendy's house.

Then my voice-over came on. "Wendy Newman begins her day at six in the morning and has to be at the sports arena by seven-thirty." On the screen it showed Wendy kissing her grandmother and leaving home.

I decided to stay on the staircase for the entire video so I wouldn't be distracted from what I had to say. I watched the monitor. During the workout the cameramen got some great shots of Wendy enjoying the physical challenge and me looking like I wanted to collapse. It was funny.

Kathleen and Cory came into the studio, and Lauren told us to move to the director's chairs. "Thirty seconds," she said. "Then discuss what you just saw a bit, then go right into the movie review."

This time I had real difficulty getting into my chair. Just as the Wendy Newman piece was coming to an end, Cory picked me up and placed me in my chair. Lauren waved him to hurry up. Then, as he hopped back on his own seat, he and his chair fell straight back. He landed with a thud as Jim pointed to us to tell us we were back on the air.

In the monitor there was a picture of us, with Cory lying on the floor. None of us knew what to say. It was a disaster. A few tense seconds crawled by.

Finally Cory jumped up and picked up his chair. "Boy!" he said. "That Wendy knocked me out of my seat!"

Kathleen and I laughed as Cory settled himself into his chair. Then Kathleen asked me what Wendy was like in person.

"She's very down-to-earth," I said. "But very disciplined with her training. She's really serious about the Olympics."

"She must be," Cory said. "I mean, to move away from home at such a young age."

"She told me it was the hardest thing she ever did."

"We all wish her luck," Kathleen said. "Lots of it."

Cory looked into the camera. "Now here's a clip from *Class Secrets*, which opens today all across the country. The movie stars Timothy Larson and Jenny Fitzgerald, and it's rated PG. Take a look."

While the short clip played, we all laughed at the falling chair incident.

"Great recovery, Cory," Kathleen said. "How did you think of that so fast?"

He shrugged. "Fear makes you say some strange things."

Back on the air we all took turns giving our review of the movie. I had no trouble with mine since I had written it out the other day and memorized what I was going to say.

"The movie is funny and touching," Kathleen said. She was the last to go. "It's just like real life. The three of us discussed it and we give it a B-plus grade. So if you get the chance, check it out this weekend. We'll be back after this commercial break with our exclusive Billy Denim interview."

As soon as we were off the air we took off running out of the studio and down the hallway toward our dressing rooms. We all had to do a major wardrobe change in only one and a half minutes.

I had already undone the belt when I got there. Mom, Jeanette, and CJ were on hand to help out. A few seconds later the hair stylist showed up, and as I pulled on my jeans she combed my hair back into a ponytail.

Kathleen had a real hard time squeezing into her jeans. She actually had to lie on the floor to work them up.

"Didn't you try them on?" I asked.

"Yeah, but I like them tight."

"Thirty seconds," CJ announced.

Kathleen jumped up and as she fastened her jeans the hair stylist put her hair in a ponytail as well. We were both wearing black jeans and white T-shirts with white bandannas through the belt loops.

We ran back to the studio. Cory was already on the little staircase. He was dressed just like we were except his bandanna was wrapped around his head like Billy Denim's had been. And he was holding an electric guitar, which was already hooked up to an amplifier.

We had barely taken our places and attached our microphones before the theme music was playing.

"Nice outfit, Cory," Kathleen said when the music faded. "Who are you supposed to be?"

"Come on, you know. I'm thinking about trying out for the band." He played some harsh-sounding noise on the guitar. "Think I'll make it?"

I shook my head. "Billy Denim you are not!"

"Okay, okay. I can take a hint. I guess we'd better show the real Billy Denim, then."

Before the actual interview they played a lot of little clips of him onstage before a crowd of screaming fans. Kathleen gave Cory and me hugs because she had to go outside for her Listen Up! segment. We wouldn't see her again until the show was over. CJ handed Kathleen a white jacket with "Friday Afternoon" printed on the back and they were off.

Cory and I sat and watched the rest of the Billy Denim segment. Mike had done such a great job editing it that nobody could tell how horribly Billy had treated us or how much he didn't want to be interviewed. He came across as a cool yet nice guy.

"Were you nervous meeting him, Delaney?" Cory asked me on the air.

"You know I was. My hands have never been so sweaty before. What about you?"

"I was cool." He picked up his guitar. "Want to hear me play another song?"

"No! That's all right. Besides, we have to get in touch with Kathleen now. She's down outside the building. Are you there, Kathleen?"

Her picture appeared on the monitor. She was outside holding a microphone with a whole group of kids standing behind her waving at the camera. "Cory, Delaney, I'm standing in Times Square, the heart of New York City. And we want you to—"

The boys and girls behind her shouted together, "Listen up!" Then they all laughed.

Kathleen seemed to be really enjoying herself. She *was* the right choice for this assignment. "Okay, listen up. The question I want to ask today is 'What do you look for when you choose new friends?' "

She pointed the microphone toward a teenage boy. "I play a lot of sports," he said. "So I usually get along with people who have a lot of the same interests. That way we can hang out after games."

Kathleen nodded and pointed the microphone toward a few other people. Some of them had strange answers. Then a little girl stepped up in front of the camera and said, "There's a new girl in my class this year, and everyone thinks she's stuck-up, but I know she's just shy. So I talked to her and she's really nice. I'm shy, too."

Kathleen laughed. "You must not be that shy. You seem perfectly calm and you're on television with millions of people watching."

The girl's face turned totally red. "I am?"

Everyone in the group laughed. Kathleen turned back toward the camera and said, "Cory and Delaney, what about you? How do you choose new friends?"

Cory thought about it for a moment. "I don't know. I get along best with funny people."

"Me too," I said. "Sense of humor is very important, but I also like people who are just plain nice. It's hard to pick new friends sometimes."

In the television monitor the camera cut back to Kathleen. She said, "The bottom line is that friendship is really special, but you have to work at it a lot. You and I know that, don't we, Delaney?"

I nodded. "But as you said, once the work is done it can be pretty special."

"Well, that's it from down here," Kathleen said.

"And that's it for the show today," Cory added. "We're

going to leave you today with the premiere of the new Billy Denim video 'Prime-time Girl.' "

I waved. "See you next week. Enjoy the rest of your Friday afternoon."

The loud crashing sound of the new Billy Denim song filled the studio, and Cory and I hugged.

"We did it!" he said. "We did it!"

I laughed. "Time to party!"

· · · · · · ·

The wrap party began about a half hour after the show had ended. We had scrubbed off all that yucky makeup and changed back into our own clothes. Then we all met in the hallway feeling comfortable and relieved.

Lauren and Mike were already in the rehearsal room with the producers and the camera crew, eating and drinking. They applauded us when we walked in, and we applauded everyone back. After all, without them there wouldn't have been any "Friday Afternoon."

After the party Lauren took us aside. "I have to say, you were all wonderful today. There were a few little glitches, but you came through it like the professionals you are."

Then she gave us our info packs for the following week. I was doing A Day in the Life of a Supermodel for the next show.

Mom gave me a hug in the elevator. "There are no words for what I'm feeling," she said. "I wish your father was here to share this moment."

So did I.

18

When we got out of the taxi, I handed Mom my knapsack and raced up the street to Kelly's house. I couldn't wait to hear what she thought of the show. I hoped she had liked it.

Kelly opened the door. "A star is born!" she said, letting me in. "May I have your autograph?"

I laughed. "Oh please."

We hugged. "You were fantastic, Laney. I was so nervous for you, but you were totally relaxed."

"That's what you think!"

Just then Mr. O'Shea stuck his head through the kitchen doorway. "Are you and Tasha finished in the kitchen, Kel? Your mom wants to get started on dinner."

"Dad!" Kelly said, pointing to me.

Mr. O'Shea looked embarrassed. "Oh, Delaney. I didn't know you were here." He turned to Kelly. "Sorry, honey."

When he left, I wanted to ask what was going on, but

I knew. Here I was thinking my friendship with Kelly was special, but it wasn't. "You're cooking with *Tasha* now?" I asked. "That's what *we* used to do together."

"Uh, w-we . . ." Kelly stammered. "It's not what you think."

"How do you know what I think? I *thought* you were my friend." I ripped off my friendship bracelet and the beads flew all over the room. "I actually wore that on television so you would see it."

"You're acting like a total jerk, Laney." She ripped hers off, too. For a few seconds we stared at each other angrily. Then I started to leave but came back. First I had to give Tasha a piece of my mind.

I stormed into the kitchen shouting, "Tasha, you sneak!"

But when I saw what she was doing, I felt like a complete idiot. She was standing at the counter putting the finishing touches on a chocolate cake. In the pink icing she had written, "Nice job, Laney."

She looked up at me and our eyes met for a second. I didn't know what to say, so I turned and ran from the kitchen and from the house without looking back.

I opened the door to my apartment and screamed, "Mom! I have to talk to you!"

"We're in the den," she called out.

We?

I went into the den where you-know-who was standing holding a bouquet of flowers. "These are for you," he said, handing them to me.

For a second I couldn't talk. I was afraid of what I might say.

Mom said, "Aren't you going to thank him?"

"Thanks, Dr. Cahill," I said, flatly.

I left the room with the stupid flowers and went down the hall to my room. Without looking, I threw them against the opposite wall as hard as I could. There was a crash.

By the time Mom and Dr. Cahill reached my room I was kneeling on the floor picking up the pieces of shattered glass. My special family photograph lay on the floor beside me.

"Be careful," Mom said. "I'll get the broom."

Before she left, Dr. Cahill said, "Lisa, let me talk to her alone."

"Okay," she said. "I'll be back in a few minutes."

Dr. Cahill came into the room. "Is the photograph damaged?"

"What difference does it make to you?"

He stood over me and looked down at the picture. "You must miss your father very much," he said.

The pain rose in my chest. "Yeah, I do."

There was a long silence, then he said, "Laney, I want you to know that I would never try to take his place."

I wanted to tell him that there was no way he ever could, but I knew it would come out wrong. He was trying to be nice. "I know."

"But I love your mother very much. You're going to have to accept that, because I'm not going anywhere."

I didn't say anything. I just stared down at the shattered glass surrounded by the broken flowers.

Mom came back into the room with the broom and asked if everything was okay. "I think so," Dr. Cahill said. "But something tells me I'm not the only problem here." They kissed. "I'll show myself out."

When he had gone, Mom cleaned up the glass in silence, then sat on the floor next to me. "Do you want to talk?"

Did I ever! I wanted to apologize to Mom and tell her that I hadn't meant to hurt Dr. Cahill's feelings. I wanted to let her know all about the fights Tasha and I had been having all summer and tell her what a fool I had been over at Kelly's. Mom would know what to do. I guess I still wanted her to be able to solve my problems for me, but deep down I knew I had to fix this mess for myself.

Instead I looked up at Mom and asked, "What was it like when you and Dad were dating?"

She smiled. "It was wonderful. You know that we met in college. He lived a few doors down from me in our dormitory, and he was always knocking on my door to ask me how to wash clothes, how to cook something, how to iron. Your grandmother did nothing to prepare him to live on his own."

"If she had, you two might not have met," I said.

"You have a point there. But we had a great time at school. We used to go jogging together every morning. We would study together and go to the movies whenever we could afford it. I have very fond memories of those years."

"Is it the same way with Dr. Cahill?"

"No, it's not the same. Nothing could ever be that way. But I'm not the same either. Your father made me the happiest person alive, and when he died I didn't know how I would ever go on. You were only seven years old and I was still in dental school. It was scary . . . very scary."

"But we survived."

"I know. And it wasn't easy. But the point is, I've

changed over the last few years. And I don't want you to compare my love for Joshua with my love for your father because there is no way to measure it. True love is true love." She looked me in the eye. "Do you understand?"

I nodded, finally getting the message. I wanted to ask her if she was happy, but I could see in her eyes that she was. And as Bryce put it, that was all that mattered.

·······

Early the next morning I called Wendy. I couldn't wait to tell her that we would soon be classmates. But she was so excited about the segment we did on her, I could barely get in a word.

"My parents called me last night and they loved it, too," she said.

"You were a great person to interview," I said. "Oh yeah, how come you weren't in school yesterday?"

"I wasn't feeling well so . . . Hey, how did you know I wasn't there?"

I started laughing. "Because I was there registering. I start Monday. Why didn't you tell me you went to the Saxon School?"

"You didn't ask!"

We both giggled.

"This is super," she said. "I haven't made any friends there yet. I'm not good at meeting people. Back in Indiana I had the same friends forever."

"You must really miss them."

"I do. Last month I ran up my grandmother's phone bill so big she told me I can only call my parents from now on."

"You can still write your friends."

"Yes, but it's not the same. You don't know what it's like losing friends."

Oh yes I did.

Before we hung up, Wendy invited me to a competition she was in the following Sunday at Madison Square Garden. She said I could invite whoever I wanted, but she had to know how many tickets I needed by that night.

"Won't I make you nervous?" I asked.

"Nah. I like having friends there for support."

"Okay. I'll call you tonight."

After we hung up I got dressed and made myself breakfast. While I ate I flipped through the *Daily News*. I couldn't believe it when I saw a review of our show. The headline read FRIDAY AFTERNOON KICKS OFF.

I read it eagerly. The first few paragraphs simply detailed the segments of the show and from what I could see the reporter really enjoyed it. But the neatest part came farther down: "Kathleen Sutherland, Cory Drennen, and Delaney Crawford are particularly talented young people and a pleasure to watch."

The doorbell rang and I answered it. Dr. Cahill was standing out in the hallway holding a package wrapped in gift paper. "Hi," I said.

He handed me the package. "I want you to have this."

"For me? Come in."

He stepped into the apartment. "Is your mother awake?"

"She's meditating. Do you want to speak to her?"

"No, no. Don't disturb her. Bryce is waiting for me in the car. We're going uptown to a place called The Lily

Pad. He wants to buy something to surprise me with."

I smiled to myself, wondering how Dr. Cahill would like living with a two-foot iguana.

I turned the package over a few times before opening it. Inside the wrapping paper was a new picture frame, trimmed in white wood. "Thanks, Dr. Cahill. This is really pretty."

"I felt responsible for what happened to the last one."

"It wasn't your fault."

"I just hope we can be friends from now on," he said.

I nodded and smiled. "We can be."

When he had gone I went into my room and placed the picture in the new frame. It fit perfectly. I hung it back on the nail, then stood back to admire it. A few days ago I never would have considered putting Dad's picture in a frame from Dr. Cahill.

Mom came into my room.

"Dr. Cahill was here," I told her. "Look what he gave me."

"I hope you thanked him properly."

"I did." I grabbed my knapsack off the closet doorknob. "Mom, I'll be right back. I have to go to the store."

"Is everything okay?"

"Everything's fine. Don't worry." I left the apartment before she could ask too many questions.

• • • • • • •

A half hour later, as I walked back up my block, I could see Tasha and Kelly playing in front of Kelly's house. I didn't know what I would say to them, but I had to do something. After my behavior yesterday, I knew it was up to me to make things right again. As I approached, they stopped what they were doing and for a while we just stood there looking at each other.

"There was a sale at the arts and crafts store," I said. Kelly folded her arms. "So?"

"I found some real pretty things." I opened the bag and pulled out a handful of tiny beads. They were in assorted colors, and they looked like marble. "I thought we could all make friendship bracelets together this time."

Neither of them said anything. I couldn't breathe. Suppose they told me to get lost?

Then Tasha reached into the bag. "We can make Kelly's bracelet this color," she said, holding up a pink bead with yellow lines in it.

I sighed, relieved. "Perfect." We looked at each other and smiled.

"Let's get started," Kelly said. "This will be fun."

Before I knew it we were headed into Kelly's house, all three of us together. I was so happy. They hadn't said a word about what had happened the night before.

We went into Kelly's room and sat on her bed. She had put up the rest of those posters. "This is great," I said. "What does your mother think of all these guys on your wall?"

"She said her little girl is growing up."

Tasha and I worked together on Kelly's bracelet first. We picked out the beads we wanted, then I held the string as she threaded them through. I looked at her face while she concentrated on what she was doing. She was absolutely beautiful. Maybe I'd always be a little jealous, but I just couldn't let it affect our friendship.

"Oh no," Kelly said. "I just thought of something. Now that we're all friends again, Laney's going to another school."

"I forgot about that," Tasha said. "We're never going to see you anymore."

"I get off work at four-thirty now," I said. "Maybe we can do our homework together sometimes. And I'll be free most weekends. Oh, that reminds me. The girl I did my segment on, Wendy, invited me to a skating competition next Saturday. Do you want to come? Free tickets."

"I'll ask my mother," Tasha said.

"Me too."

"Great." It felt good to be making plans with them again.

When all three bracelets were done, I reached into the bag for the surprise I had bought. "Close your eyes and open your hands," I said.

They giggled and followed my orders. The store I had gone to had a whole table of really cute charms. I hadn't been able to resist them. I gave one kitten charm to Tasha, one to Kelly, and kept one for myself.

"Okay, open your eyes."

"How cute," Kelly said. "Charms for our bracelets."

We put the bracelets on one another. They looked nice with the three kittens dangling with our every movement.

"Now we have to promise to be friends for life," Kelly said. "No matter what."

All three of us held up the hand with the bracelet and promised at the same time. I had a good feeling, like this time nothing would get in the way of our friendship.

Then Tasha jumped up. "Oh, I get it. The three little

kittens. Our silly camp play." Then she started prancing around the room with a sad expression on her face and sang, "We're the three little kittens who lost our mittens."

Kelly and I stood up and joined in with her. "And we don't know where to find them." We shook our pretend tails, then we fell on the bed laughing like old friends.